SCHOOL CLOTHES

SCHOOL CLOTHES

When You're Not Old Enough for the "Regular" Summer Job

By Linda Carlysle Clarke

School Clothes – When you're not old enough for the "regular" summer job

Author: Linda Carlysle Clarke

Cover Design: Linda Carlysle Clarke

This novel is a work of fiction. Any resemblance to actual persons (living or deceased) or reference to real people, events, songs, or business establishments or locales is purely coincidental.
ISBN: 979-8-9899445-0-7

First Printing 2024

Printed in the United States

DEDICATIONS

Giving honor to God, the Creator; Jesus the Christ; and the Holy Spirit my daily comfort and guide as I finally put pen to paper for the writing of my inaugural novel which has been twirling in my head for several decades.

To Dirk (aka Derrek) and Nusara, QIV (aka Carl) and J'Breana for your unconditional love and support.

Much love to my family and to my friends' circle who knowingly and unknowingly supported me through this writing journey.

To Quashon Davis, author and mentor. I am forever grateful for your guidance through the publication process. May blessings continue to flow in your life.

PREFACE

Remember that summer when everything changed? We've all been there, and for young teenage Laura, it was the summer of 1980. It was Laura's transition summer from junior high to high school. Everybody around her was excited about their summer break, with plans of working part-time at the local mall or fast-food joints, playing a little recreational league softball, even a few drives to the lake or Myrtle Beach.

But not Laura; she was preoccupied with trying to figure out how to get enough money to purchase new school clothes that actually fit her slim frame. The young teen had pretty much floated through junior high in obscurity, or so she thought, wearing her aunt's ill-fitting, hand-me-down, adult-looking clothes.

As it had been since kindergarten, with her late September birthday, Laura was always a year younger than her peer group. And here it was, only two months before starting high school and fourteen-year-old Laura found herself too young for a work permit. Determined to earn some money and purchase new school clothes, Laura embarks on a summer adventure beyond her imagination.

OH, WHAT TO DO?

There was excitement in the air as the bright yellow school bus pulled up to the intersection of Timberwood Street and Elwood Road. Everybody was laughing and talking about summer break. That is, everybody except Laura. Stepping off the school bus, officially ending her last day of junior high school, Laura barely heard all the chatter going on around her. The young teen's thoughts were not on summer fun but on how to make some money for new school clothes. To her, the first day of high school was approaching fast. Laura walked down Timberwood toward her Grandma Annie's house so engrossed in thought, she didn't even hear her best friend Sydney shout out to her, wave goodbye, and turn to walk down the opposite end of Timberwood.

Laura approached the light gray wooden frame house with her thoughts still occupied with what to do for the summer to make some money. She had been looking for a job since April, but no one would hire the fourteen-year-old teenager. Laura's mama had told her that over the summer, she could fix up some clothes Aunt Nicky had brought over to the house. There was no way she was going to start high school wearing Aunt Nicky's hand-me-down clothes, like she had worn all through junior high. Laura knew her mama didn't have any extra money with taking care of all of them, but still there had to be a better option than starting high school wearing oversized old blouses with rolled-up sleeves and baggy, hemmed-up pants. She was determined to find a summer job.

"Hey, Grandma Annie, I'm here," Laura shouted out as she entered the front door into her grandma's living room.

Her younger sister, Danielle, jumped up from the couch, greeting her with a furor of energy. The lil girl barely took a breath as she rattled off the happenings of her last day of third grade. Laura actually lived two streets over on Pinewood Street. She had to pick up her lil sis from their grandma's house because by the time school let out, their mama was already at work for the evening shift at the factory. Miss Cora, mama's ride, usually picked her up around 3:00 p.m. for the 3:30 p.m. to midnight shift.

"Hi, Laura, how was your last day of junior high?" Grandma Annie greeted her coming into the room, peering over the little wire frame glasses sitting on the tip of her nose.

"It was good, but I still haven't found a summer job," Laura pouted.

"Well, don't worry, something will come, maybe you can bag or stock down at that grocery store where your brother, John, works," Grandma Annie encouraged her.

"No, he already asked, and I'm not old enough," Laura sighed.

Today was her older brother John's last day of eleventh grade; he was officially a senior. John had probably gone straight to the A&P Grocery Store after school. Between sports, he worked there bagging groceries and stocking. Laura speculated that with school being out for the summer, he would probably work a lot more hours.

Changing the subject, her grandma offered Laura something to eat. Laura declined, knowing that her mama had left food in the refrigerator for them. It just needed to be warmed up.

Helping Danielle gather her backpack, the two girls said their goodbyes to Grandma Annie and quickly walked the two blocks home. Danielle took off running toward the little grayish-blue wood frame house as they turned the corner on to Pinewood Street. Entering the living room, Laura turned the television on to *Scooby-Doo*—her lil sis's favorite show. She then headed down the hallway toward the bedroom they both shared, still pondering what to do.

The first two weeks of summer break had gone by painstakingly slow for Laura. Most of her time was spent babysitting Danielle. Laura and Sydney had gone to the mall a couple of times, but no one was willing to hire the two underage teens. She leaned back on the pillows propped up against her headboard. It was Monday, the start of another week and still no job in sight. It was the end of June already, and time was ticking.

She heard her mama shout down the hallway, "Laura, I'm leaving."

Laura peeped out the window and saw Miss Cora's brown Chevrolet Impala pull into the driveway. She got up to go check on Danielle in the living room and heard the phone ringing. Laura picked the phone handle up from its cradle on the little side table.

"Hey, girl, what you doing?" Sydney greeted Laura.

"Nothing much, getting ready to watch some television with Danielle," Laura answered while taking a seat on the couch.

"Well," Sydney continued, "there is a man at my church, Mr. Isaiah. His family has a tobacco farm out in the country in this little town called Herd. It's about thirty miles outside the city. I overheard some people at church talking about how Mr. Isaiah sometimes hires a few teens to work on his farm during the summer to help bring in the tobacco crop."

Interrupting Sydney, Laura exclaimed incredulously, "Girl, please, I'm not getting ready to work on no farm picking tobacco in this North Carolina heat! This is 1980, not 1880!"

Sydney laughed and continued explaining that they would not be picking no tobacco. From what she had heard, the women work in a covered barn area to tie and hang the tobacco up for drying before it's taken to market. She assured Laura that it was easy work, and they would get paid in cash every Friday.

Laura's interest peaked at the sound of cash every Friday. Sydney's parents had already agreed that she and her brother, Jacob, could work provided Mr. Isaiah agreeing to hire them.

"My dad is going to talk to him on Sunday after church. So, you need to let me know by Saturday night," Sydney urged Laura.

"OK, I'll let you know. I'll talk to you later, bye." Laura hung up the phone mulling over the prospect of easy work and cash every Friday. She had never been in the country and knew nothing about tobacco.

After watching a couple of episodes of *Scooby-Doo* with Danielle, Laura went into the kitchen. How hard could it be, she thought, taking the hamburger and noodle casserole out of the refrigerator to warm for dinner. Now to convince her mama.

Laura decided that Saturday morning while her mama was having coffee would be the best time to talk to her about working on the tobacco farm. She had the coffee pot perking and had already put a load of clothes in the washer by the time her mama got up and came into the kitchen. It actually didn't take as much convincing as the young teenager had thought it would. Her mama knew Sydney's parents and was agreeable to letting Laura work once she heard that Sydney and her brother, Jacob, would also be working on the farm. Danielle would continue to go to Grandma Annie's house in the afternoon, and Laura would pick her up in the evenings when she got home from the tobacco farm.

The only stipulation was that Laura had to give a portion of her pay to her mama to help with the household bills. Laura was OK with that, as if she had a choice. She already knew her brother, John, gave Mama a portion of his paycheck, but she didn't know how much. John had opened a savings account at the local bank, but Laura was having none of that. She was getting paid in cash and planned to spend her money on new school clothes. After getting the OK from her mama, Laura went to call Sydney.

On most Sundays, Laura and her family ate dinner at Grandma Annie's house. Her grandma was a great cook who still made homemade biscuits that melted in your mouth. Laura's mama usually fried up a batch of chicken to go with the Sunday meal. Grandma Annie had everybody laughing about something that had happened at church. Laura didn't even hear the story because she was anxious for dinner to be over so that she could go to Sydney's house. She looked around the table. Her grandma was a short, thickset woman with a ready smile. You could tell she used to be much smaller in her younger days. Their Grandpa Larry had passed away years ago when Laura was a little girl. She could barely remember him, except that he was really tall. Grandma Annie kept an old black-and-white photo of him on the side table in the living room. Come to think of it, Laura remembered being told that her name was a variation of her grandpa's name. Her mama was tall and slender. And then there was her mama's sister, Aunt Nicky. Laura looked at her aunt. She was kinda short, like Grandma Annie, and very slender. That's probably why she got all of Aunt Nicky's old clothes, Laura thought to herself as the conversation continued around the dinner table.

As soon as Sunday dinner was over, Laura walked down to Sydney's house, which was on the same street past the intersection. It was a little after 4:00 p.m., and the sun was still shining bright as Laura approached the light green house trimmed in white. Sydney must have been watching from the window because she came bouncing out the front door as soon as Laura started up the steps. She grabbed Laura's hand and pulled her toward the two white rocking chairs on the far end of the porch.

"Girl!" Sydney greeted her full of enthusiasm and with a big grin. "It's all set up; we start tomorrow morning!"

"What, for real!" Laura screamed with joy and immediately started firing out questions. "How do we get to the farm? What do we have to wear? And most importantly, how much are we getting paid?"

Sydney started explaining the plan for working on the tobacco farm. The teens would begin work tomorrow, Monday, July 7th, and work for six weeks until August 15th. Mr. Isaiah was going to pick them up in front of her house at 7:00 a.m. for the drive to the farm and then bring them back in the afternoon around 6:00 p.m. In addition to Sydney's brother, Jacob, their friends Mike and Amy were also going to be working on the tobacco farm with them. Laura knew Amy because she was in their English class. She also knew Mike because he played ball with her brother. They both lived down the opposite end of Timberwood Street.

"Oh, and my mom said that we just need to wear an old shirt and an old pair of jeans. Something that we don't mind getting dirty," Sydney said and laughed.

"OK, OK," Laura interrupted her. "But most importantly, how much are we getting paid?"

Sydney continued, "Girl, Mr. Isaiah is going to pay us $200 in cash every Friday!"

"Two hundred dollars a week for six weeks; that's $1,200!" Laura shouted out gleefully.

The girls were talking and laughing so much that Sydney's mom, Mrs. Wilson, came to the front screen door and stepped out onto the porch to check on them. Laura thanked her profusely for getting them the summer jobs working on the tobacco farm.

"Well don't thank me just yet," Mrs. Wilson laughed. "It will be a good learning experience for you all." She went back inside to get the girls some lemonade.

Learning experience, Laura thought to herself, I'm not trying to learn a lot about no tobacco farm. I'm just trying to get paid! The girls continued chatting for another hour or so about finally getting a summer job and their shopping plans for those Friday cash payments.

Laura walked back down the street to her Grandma Annie's house and arrived just in time for homemade chocolate cake. They all sat outside on the front porch eating chocolate cake and vanilla ice cream as the slightest summer breeze started to fill the afternoon air. Her brother, John, had left a few hours ago, before dessert, to hang out with friends. Aunt Nicky was already gone also. Laura took a seat on the top step and began to give her mama and grandma the update about Mr. Isaiah agreeing to let them work on his tobacco farm. Both women were a little surprised that it was starting the very next day.

Grandma Annie commented to Laura, "This summer should be very interesting since you have never been out to the country, much less worked on a tobacco farm."

That didn't matter to Laura. She was too excited about finally getting a paid job. She was even going to be able to work and hang out with her best friend, Sydney, at the same time.

As the sun started to set, Laura's mama had them clean up Grandma Annie's kitchen and pack some leftovers for Monday's dinner. Laura, her mama, and Danielle walked back home to get ready for Monday morning, the start of a new workweek. Laura was beyond happy.

While Danielle was taking her bath, Laura started to lay out her clothes for work. It was going to be a very early 6:00 a.m. start tomorrow morning. She took out a blue tank top, a plaid blue-and-black fitted button-down shirt and a pair of knee-length blue jean shorts. Laura thought to herself, I'm not going to wear a pair of regular long jeans to work outside on a hot summer day; besides, they were not going to be in the tobacco field. After showering and getting ready for bed, Laura drifted off to sleep with visions of herself in the mall buying all sorts of new jeans, blouses, dresses, and shoes for the start of high school.

THE SUMMER JOB - FIRST WORKWEEK

JULY 7-11, 1980

Laura jumped at the sound of the blaring 6:00 a.m. alarm clock. She quickly turned it off, not wanting to wake up everyone in the small house. Their three tiny bedrooms were right across from each other along the short hallway. She glanced over at Danielle who was still sound asleep. Laura quietly walked to the shared bathroom and brushed her teeth. Looking into the mirror, she decided to pull her hair back in a ponytail because it was going to be a hot day. Laura put on the clothes she had laid out the night before, took a quick look in the mirror, and headed down the hallway toward the kitchen.

The sun was already shining through the kitchen window. Laura pulled back the curtains and looked outside; it was going to be a hot July day. The kitchen faced the backyard, and she could see the row of pine trees that separated the houses on her street from the backyards of the houses on Pinecone Road. Pinecone was the road between Laura's and Grandma Annie's streets. According to community legend, their neighborhood used to be a forest of pine cone trees, and that's how it ended up with all the tree-related names when the housing development was built. There were still pine trees everywhere, Laura mused while popping two slices of bread into the toaster and pouring herself a glass of juice. Sitting at the kitchen table contemplating her first day on the tobacco farm, the sound of the toast popping up made her jump a little.

It was not even 6:30 a.m. but Laura was dressed, finished eating her toast, and ready for her first day on the tobacco farm. It was still a bit early to take the five-minute walk to Sydney's house. She lingered at the table a few more minutes, thinking about Friday's payday and how much fun they would have on Saturday at the mall. Laura didn't want to wake up her mama to let her know that she was leaving for work, so she gently pushed the bedroom door open and peeped in. Her mama was already awake.

"Morning, Laura, you already up and ready for your first day," she greeted her.

Laura was surprised that her mama was awake. Working the night shift at the factory, she usually got in around 12:30 a.m. and didn't get up until about 9:00 or 10:00 a.m.

"Yes, ma'am, I'm getting ready to walk to Sydney's house," Laura responded.

"OK, be careful and remember to go to your grandma's house and pick up Danielle when you get back this evening," her mama said as she pulled the covers up and turned over for a few more hours of sleep.

Laura pulled the bedroom door closed and turned to walk down the hallway toward the front door. She made sure the front door was locked behind her as she walked down the steps to her first workday. The walk to Sydney's house was quick. As she approached, Laura could see Sydney, Jacob, and Mike already on the porch. Amy was coming down the sidewalk in the opposite direction.

Everybody was busy talking about what the first day on the tobacco farm was going to be like. They were so excited with anticipation that nobody noticed when the large, black, glistening truck made the right turn on to Timberwood Street until it pulled up in front of the house. A very tall, heavyset man jumped out from the driver's side. That must be Mr. Isaiah, Laura thought. He looked like a giant of a man wearing bib overalls and a wide-brim baseball cap. The man walked up to the porch and greeted the group of teens with a loud, booming voice.

"Good morning, I'm Isaiah Thompson."

Laura glanced at her watch, and it was precisely 7:00 a.m. As the teens greeted Mr. Isaiah, Mr. Wilson came out on to the front porch. With an air of familiarity, he greeted Mr. Isaiah and offered him and the other man sitting in the passenger side of the truck a cup of coffee. He called the other man Nate. Mr. Isaiah declined the coffee and exclaimed in his booming voice about the need to get out to the farm. The other man, Nate, just kinda nodded his baseball-cap-covered head in agreement.

"Are these my summer workers?" Mr. Isaiah asked.

"Yes," Mr. Wilson said, introducing Laura, Amy, and Mike. While introducing them he reminded Mr. Isaiah that Amy also attended their church. "And of course, you already know my children, Jacob and Sydney."

"OK, great, let's load up, young folks," he bellowed. "There are benches on each side in the back of the truck, no standing."

As the five teens walked down the steps and started to get up into the cargo bed of the truck, the man on the passenger side greeted them with a nod of his baseball cap. Laura heard Mr. Isaiah telling Mr. Wilson that he'd have them back by 6:00 p.m. The big man jumped back in the truck, and they were on their way to the country.

Come to think of it, Laura realized that she had never been in a truck before, and she certainly didn't think they would be riding to work in the back of a pickup truck. She silently hoped no one from the neighborhood saw them.

Laura leaned over to Sydney and whispered, "I thought we would be riding in a car or van."

"No, I knew it was going to be a truck; Mr. Isaiah always drives a truck to church," Sydney responded with a shrug of her shoulders.

Riding in the open cargo bed made it hard for the teens to talk without screaming over the breeze blowing into the back of the truck. The girls' ponytails were flying in the wind. All three girls wore jean shorts that fell just above their knees and a short-sleeve button-down shirt with a tank shirt underneath. It was as if they had decided on their own little uniforms. Jacob and Mike sat on the opposite side of the truck wearing t-shirts and long jean pants. The boys seemed to really enjoy the drive with their arms stretched out to their sides taking in the morning breeze.

Within minutes they were out of the city and driving down a paved two-lane road. In what seemed like twenty to twenty-five minutes, Mr. Isaiah took a left turn on to a rocky dirt and gravel road. The teens were bouncing up and down on the benches. The guys were cracking up laughing. There were fields on both sides of the dirt road with rows and rows of what Laura suspected was tobacco. She had never seen tobacco before, except in the form of cigarettes, cigars, and snuff. She wasn't sure if the others had been out in the country before. Sydney had never mentioned it.

Out of nowhere these huge old brown rustic barns rose up as they rounded a curve on the rocky dirt road. As the truck got closer, Laura saw another large black truck backed up to an overhang attached to the barn. Mr. Isaiah brought the truck to a stop and jumped out.

He bellowed, "Come with me, girls; you're gonna be working at this barn today."

Laura, Sydney, and Amy pensively climbed down from the cargo bed of the truck. Jacob and Mike waited in the truck and waved as the girls followed Mr. Isaiah. Three older women were already under the overhang working at a long table full of green leaves. What a sight!

"Good morning, ladies," Mr. Isaiah greeted the three women with his loud, bellowing voice.

From the looks of things, it was pretty clear the women had already been there working before the girls arrived. The truck was half empty.

Walking up to the ladies, Mr. Isaiah said, "Girls, I want you to meet Mrs. Mary, Miss Elaine, and Mrs. Cindy. You will be working with them."

The ladies had stopped working to meet their summer teen helpers. Mr. Isaiah had already told them earlier that morning that he was bringing three teen girls to work for the summer. The women were used to Mr. Isaiah bringing a couple of teen boys to help with the tobacco harvest, but this was the first time he brought teen girls. When introducing the women, Mr. Isaiah went on to explain to the teens that the ladies had been working stringing tobacco during the summer for years. According to him, they were experts at the task and would show the teen girls what to do with the tobacco. The ladies smiled and greeted the young girls as Mr. Isaiah also introduced the teens by name.

"Take good care of them. Another truckload of tobacco will be coming shortly. I'll see you all around noon for lunch break." And with those pronouncements, Mr. Isaiah was back in the truck headed down the rocky dirt road with Jacob and Mike still in the back of the truck.

Looking around, Laura saw that all three of the older women were wearing bib overalls with long-sleeve black t-shirts underneath. They also had headscarves tied around their heads. The sun was beaming already, and to Laura the women looked very hot.

The one introduced as Mrs. Mary told the girls, "It's gonna be a busy day, we need to get this load bundled up before the next truck gits here."

Mrs. Mary took the lead and instructed Laura and Sydney to stand on her side of the table and she had Amy go stand on the other side with Mrs. Cindy and Miss Elaine. She told the teens to watch Mrs. Cindy and Miss Elaine as she explained to them what the women were doing.

"You take about ten to fifteen leaves, depending on the size of the leaves, then you loop the string around the top of the stems to hold the leaves together. The string needs to be about twice the size of this here piece of wood. Then tie the bundle onto the stick. Continue looping and tying bundles until the stick is full. Then you place the full stick on that big table over there against the barn. Go take a look inside the barn."

The three teens looked in amazement. Oh wow! Tobacco was hanging on these long horizontal poles in rows from floor to ceiling. The teen girls went back to listening attentively as Mrs. Mary continued explaining the process. They learned that when this barn got full, they'd all go work at the second barn. The men came in the evenings to hang the sticks from beam to beam for drying and also to rotate out the dried tobacco. The whole process was called barning the tobacco. Eventually the dried tobacco was sold. Mr. Isaiah's tobacco farm was big enough to keep them steady busy until about mid-August, a couple of weeks before the new school year started.

Mrs. Mary told the girls, "See that little building in the back of the barn? It's an outhouse with a toilet and small sink." She continued, "Let's get started because that next truckload will be here in a minute."

The girls looked at each other with trepidation with just the thought of having to use the outhouse. As the week went on, they also quickly learned that "a minute" actually meant about thirty minutes to an hour. The work area was large enough that each person had a stick to string the tobacco. Mrs. Mary got in the middle of Laura and Sydney. Mrs. Cindy and Miss Elaine put Amy in the middle of them on the opposite side of the table. Laura and Sydney peered at each other with a slight quirky squint once they realized this setup didn't allow them to talk to each other.

Mrs. Mary's hands were moving like lighting as she finished bundling a whole stick. Laura and Sydney were just tying their sixth bundle. Each stick held about fifteen bundles. The women had already been working before the girls arrived so the load was almost done, and in about an hour, they saw another truck turning in down the dirt road. The driver was Mr. Nate, the same man who was riding with Mr. Isaiah when he picked them up that morning. Laura looked at her watch and saw that it was around 9:00 a.m.

Mr. Nate jumped out the truck. He was as tall as Mr. Isaiah but not quite as burly. He wore his ball cap pulled down over his forehead and dark sunglasses.

"Y'all ready for another load?" he greeted them.

The women and teen girls stepped back while Mr. Nate and his helper pulled out the empty truck and backed the new load up against the overhang worktable.

This was the first time the girls had a chance to huddle for a quick chat. The teens were surprised at how wet they were getting from stringing the tobacco. It was just their first truck and most of it was already done before they even got started.

A large red Igloo cooler with a package of small cups was sitting at the end of the overhang just outside the barn on a long narrow table up against the wall.

"Oh, that tastes good," Amy said with an exhale.

The water was nice and cold. Remembering the outhouse, Laura only filled her cup half full. She noticed that there were several food coolers also on the table. None of the teens had brought any lunch, assuming they would go to a fast-food place.

With the second load of tobacco, the girls were concentrating hard on stringing and attempting to do it a little faster. They didn't talk, but Mrs. Mary, Mrs. Cindy, and Miss Elaine continued their conversation while working with rhythmic speed. They barely looked down at the truckload of tobacco except to move a finished stick to the side.

As the truck bed was getting down to almost empty, Laura spoke up and said, "Mr. Nate should be here shortly; who is he?"

Miss Elaine answered, "Oh, that's Mr. Isaiah's cousin. Their fathers were brothers, both of them have passed. Those cousins pretty much grew up like brothers. They work this farm together, not sure which one owns it or if they own it together."

"Yeah, they good men," Mrs. Mary chimed in as they continued stringing the tobacco.

Laura was amazed at how these women never broke their rhythm, not even to answer her question. She and Sydney had slowed down to listen to Miss Elaine and Mrs. Mary. Amy seemed to have kept her pace. Laura looked up because she heard another truck clanking down the rocky dirt road. She checked her watch again, and it was just about 10:30 a.m. The time between truckloads had really gone by fast. Sure enough, it was Mr. Nate and his helper with another load of tobacco.

Laura and the girls were happy for another quick break because they were starting to get really dirty from handling the tobacco. It was very hot, so the dampness was drying quick but leaving dried dirt stains on their clothes and bodies, especially their arms.

Sydney exclaimed, "When my mom told me that she had worked cropping tobacco as a teenager, she never said anything about it being this wet and dirty."

"I wonder what Jacob and Mike are doing," Amy said.

The morning had been so nonstop busy that Sydney had almost forgotten about her brother and Mike. As the girls got back into position to start on the third truck, they laughed at the thought of the boys being super wet and dirty. Laura's watch was getting dirty, and she didn't want it to stop running, so she took it off and put it in the pocket of her jean shorts. The older women were steadily working with precision speed. As the girls tried to keep up, Laura heard and felt a rumble in her stomach. Those two pieces of toast were long digested, and she was getting hungry. She had $7 to get some lunch, and the money needed to last her all week. She thought to herself that she had not seen a McDonald's or any other place to get lunch as they were driving to the tobacco farm this morning.

"Here comes the fourth truck, lunchtime!" Mrs. Cindy announced.

The girls looked up toward the incoming truck. Laura pulled out her watch and checked the time, it was 12:15 p.m. A second truck turned down the road. Oh my, Laura thought, two truckloads of tobacco! But as the trucks got closer and pulled up to the barn, they saw that one truck was loaded with more tobacco and the other truck was loaded with a bunch of boys and older men. Out jumped Jacob and Mike along with the others. They were filthy dirty. Laura was thinking that she and the girls should have worn long jeans. Mr. Nate was driving the load of tobacco, and Mr. Isaiah was driving the second truck with the older men and boys.

Looking in the teens' direction, Mr. Isaiah said, "I noticed that you young people didn't bring any lunch. Do you want to ride up to Walker's Corner Store to get a drink and sandwich?"

Mrs. Mary and the ladies quickly spoke up, inviting the teens to have some of their lunch. Wanting a break, Laura and the others quickly decided to take the ride to the corner store. They climbed into the back of the truck.

"We'll be back around 1:00 p.m.," Mr. Isaiah bellowed at the crew that was staying behind.

Laura counted and six guys stayed back. Three of them looked to be around their age and the other three appeared to be older men. She had particularly noticed that one of the teen boys seemed to give a ready smile and nod toward Mrs. Cindy.

During the ride to Walker's Corner Store, the girls were shouting over the wind coming into the back of the truck, telling Jacob and Mike about their morning and asking about the guys' morning. Jacob and Mike explained that they had spent the morning walking up and down the fields loading the picked tobacco onto the back of the truck. It was wet and hot work. The tobacco plants are about four to six feet tall and wet from the overnight dew.

"We're only working about ten to fifteen minutes from the barn," Jacob said.

As Jacob was talking, Mr. Isaiah took a turn off the paved road down another long gravel road. They were only on the gravel road for a couple of minutes when the teens saw a white concrete building with a big red sign on the front that read Walker's Corner Store. There were a few trucks already parked out front as Mr. Isaiah made a slight turn and parked under a huge shade tree.

Jumping out the truck, Mr. Isaiah told them, "Y'all can rinse off your arms and hands with the hose to the side of the building before coming in to buy some lunch. We'll be here for about thirty minutes."

The five teens trekked to the side of the building. Laura and the girls washed their hands and arms, then hosed down their legs. It was so hot they dried instantly. Laura noticed that the guys' hands and arms were already clean. They must have used the field outhouse, she mused.

Everybody in the store seemed to know Mr. Isaiah and Mr. Nate. Both men purchased large fountain drinks and went back outside. The teens looked around. The little store had a few shelves with general use items along with sodas, chips, cookies, and candy. There was also a hot food section in the corner with a couple of coffee pots, hot dogs on a rolling rotisserie, and pizza. All five of them purchased a fountain drink, hot dog with fixins, and a bag of chips. The store was selling that combination as a lunch meal for $2.30.

"Wow, that's almost the cost of a Big Mac meal at McDonald's!" Laura exclaimed as they walked out the store. She only had $4 and change left for the rest of the week.

It was hot in the store and nowhere to really sit and eat. Mr. Isaiah and Mr. Nate had the truck doors open trying to catch some breeze from the big shade tree. Laura saw that they were eating sandwiches from two mini coolers.

As they climbed into the back of the truck, Laura said, "It looks like everybody brings their lunch."

"Yep, guess there's no McDonald's or Burger King out here," Amy responded.

Laura was thinking about it more from the money aspect because buying lunch at Walker's Corner Store every day would be about $12 a week of her $200 weekly shopping funds. No way, she would have to start bringing her lunch!

"Who were the other three boys working with you all?" Sydney asked her brother, Jacob.

"Two of them are brothers named David Jr. and Daniel, and the other one is Anthony." Jacob responded. He continued, "Their fathers were two of the men who came in on the truck for lunch. They all live out here in Herd and go to the same high school."

Laura was listening intently and wondering which of the three teen boys was the one she saw nodding at Mrs. Cindy with the nice smile. Just as it was starting to feel good relaxing and talking about the morning's activities, Mr. Isaiah announced that he's getting ready to head back to the barn.

He also bellowed out to this big red truck, "OK, fellas, I'll see you back at the field."

"Those are the other men who work in the tobacco field with us," Mike explained to the girls.

The truck pulled back up to the barn, and Mr. Nate got out of the passenger side to go and drive the empty truck back out to the field. The girls jumped out of the back of the truck. Their bodies were starting to feel the morning workout from stringing three truckloads of tobacco. Laura watched as the three teen boys ran and got into the back of the truck with Jacob and Mike. One of the men got into the passenger side of the empty truck with Mr. Nate. The other man got into the passenger side of the truck with Mr. Isaiah while the third man hopped into the back with the teens. She wondered which two were brothers. Her eyes rested again on the boy with the dimpled smile. Oh, he seemed to look in her direction; did he notice her staring at them? Laura thought to herself that the three of them must look a sight to the group with their dirty blue jean shorts, shirts, and their sweaty, frizzed ponytails. She understood why the women wore cotton bandanas tied around their heads because all morning the sweat was steadily pouring down her face even though they were working under the overhang.

Sydney interrupted her thoughts, "Come on, Laura, Mrs. Mary and them are ready to get started on this truckload of tobacco."

The girls all laughed as they got in position to begin stringing the fourth truck of the day. It was about 1:15 p.m. As they began stringing, Mrs. Mary asked about the girls' lunch break down at Walker's. The girls complained about the limited choices of a hot dog or a slice of pizza. They had thought there would be a McDonald's or a Burger King close by.

All three women burst into laughter as Mrs. Mary told them, "The closest fast-food restaurant is in Ervinsville, your hometown, about thirty miles up the road."

Laura said, "I guess we'll have to start bringing our lunch."

Sydney and Amy nodded their heads in agreement. Mrs. Cindy explained that everyone brought their lunch. Her husband was Mr. David Ingram, and her two sons were David Jr. and Daniel. The girls also found out through conversation that Mrs. Mary's husband was named Roy Smith and one of the teens was their son, Anthony. The third man was Kevin James. The women teased that he comes back to the barn for lunch because he's sweet on Elaine. Mrs. Mary and Mrs. Cindy winked at each other across the table and gave out a good-natured laugh. Miss Elaine admonished the women, insisting that he's just a friend.

"Yeah, right," Mrs. Mary and Mrs. Cindy say in unison as their hands continue rhythmically stringing the tobacco.

The three women had been friends for years and were at ease with the good-natured teasing. They worked in the Herd Elementary School cafeteria. During the summer, their families worked on the tobacco farm to make some extra money. The women continued stringing and chatting. Laura and the girls mostly listened as they tried to get a steady stringing rhythm.

Like clockwork, around 3:00 p.m., another truck was turning down the little dirt road. Laura thought, how can this tobacco still be so damp this far into the day? Granted it wasn't as wet as the morning loads, but the girls were still getting pretty wet and dirty. After those sodas for lunch, the girls couldn't take it anymore and had to venture to the outhouse during the truck swap out. The outhouse was much cleaner than the teen girls expected it to be.

But it was still kinda creepy. Laura made a note to herself not to drink a large soda for lunch anymore.

They settled in working on the fifth truck, and Mrs. Mary explained to the girls how the afternoon would flow. This would be the last truckload of tobacco for the day. When the guys come back around 5:00 p.m., they would switch the trucks out so that there was a load of tobacco ready to start stringing first thing tomorrow morning. The girls were happy to hear that news because they were ready to go home and have some nice long, hot showers.

"Y'all have done really good for a first day," Mrs. Mary commended them.

The women continued working and their conversation turned toward what they were fixing for dinner. It appeared Sunday leftovers were a Monday meal for a lot of people. Laura was starting to feel the tiredness of standing since early morning. The muscles in her arms and hands were definitely starting to ache. They were nonstop busy for the next couple of hours, trying to finish up the last truckload of tobacco for the day.

As they were finishing stringing the last bit of tobacco, Laura saw three trucks turning down the dirt road. She took out her watch, and it was 5:15 p.m. Mr. Isaiah sure has this work timed exact, she thought to herself. Sure enough, Mr. Nate was driving one truck laden down with tobacco. Mr. Isaiah was driving the pretty, black, glistening truck with the benches in the back. One of the other men was driving a large, dark blue pickup truck.

Mr. Isaiah jumped out of the truck, greeting them with his booming voice, "How was your first day?"

"It was good," the girls all responded in unison, even though their little bodies were exhausted.

Mrs. Mary chimed in. "They're doing really good, picking it up fast, by the end of the week they'll be bundling tobacco like pros."

Everybody laughed. Mrs. Mary gathered the teens together to introduce the boys and girls as the men swapped out the last truck. Anthony and Daniel were juniors at Herd High School. David Jr.

was a senior. The boys had been friends since elementary school, just like Laura and Sydney.

Sydney spoke up and introduced her brother, Jacob, and friend, Mike, to the women. Laura thought to herself, so it's Daniel with the nice, dimpled smile. They were old enough for work permits. She wondered why they were working in tobacco. She looked at Sydney and Amy—they looked a dirty sight—and Laura knew that she looked the same as they all greeted the teen boys. The boys wore bib overalls with long-sleeve black t-shirts. Their clothes were pretty dirty too, but at least their arms and legs were covered. That must be the unspoken uniform, Laura mused as the five teens jumped into the cargo bed of Mr. Isaiah's truck.

As Mr. Isaiah was pulling off, Laura watched as Mrs. Cindy got into the cab of the dark blue truck with Mr. David Ingram, and she scooted over so that Miss Elaine could get in also. David Jr., Daniel, and Mr. Kevin jumped into the back of the truck. Mr. Roy Smith got into the truck with Mr. Nate and moved over, making room for Mrs. Mary. Anthony jumped in the back. They all must live in the same neighborhood, Laura thought, not knowing that none of them lived in a community of houses like what she was used to in the city.

The ride back to Ervinsville seemed to go by quickly. The teens were so tired from the day's work that they just sat back and soaked in the breeze blowing into the back of the truck. By the time Mr. Isaiah pulled up in front of Sydney's house, Jacob and Mike were asleep. Laura looked at her watch; it was just about 6:00 p.m.

Sydney's mom, Mrs. Wilson, came out on the porch just as the truck pulled up. She had been looking out the window waiting for them to return from their first day on the tobacco farm. "Hey, Isaiah, how did they do today?" she greeted him.

"They were just fine," he responded. "By the end of the week, they'll have the full swing of things." He never turned off his truck as they exchanged greetings while Laura and the teen crew jumped out of the back of the truck. "I'll see you young folks at 7:00 a.m.

tomorrow morning," he shouted and was on his way back to the country.

Laura wondered if he had to go back to the barn to take out the dried tobacco and hang the tobacco they strung today. She couldn't imagine having to work another hour...it had been a very long day.

"Whew!" Mrs. Wilson greeted them. "You all look like you need some hot showers to clean off that dried dirt."

Everybody laughed in agreement. Jacob hopped up the steps past his mom.

"Take off those dirty shoes!" she shouted.

While Jacob took off his shoes, Mike told Mrs. Wilson about their experience loading tobacco in the back of trucks all day. Jacob told everyone goodbye, left his shoes on the porch, and went inside to beat Sydney to the shower. Mike headed up the sidewalk toward home. Looking at how dirty the girls' jean shorts and legs were, Mrs. Wilson reminded them that she had recommended they wear blue jean pants.

"Yes, ma'am," Laura responded. "We thought shorts would be good since it was going to be so hot. But we're definitely going to wear blue jean pants tomorrow."

Amy said, "Too bad we don't have any bib overalls like Mrs. Mary and the other women."

"Girl, they looked hot, and with those long-sleeve black t-shirts..." Laura continued.

"Well, I know it's hot standing out here on this sidewalk," Sydney interjected. "I'll see you all in the morning." She turned to go up the porch steps.

Mrs. Wilson had been standing there just smiling as she listened to the young girls talk about their first day ever working a paid job and on a tobacco farm at that. Laura headed down the street toward her Grandma Annie's house. She was glad that it was just a few houses down from Sydney's because she didn't want to be seen by anybody.

Laura walked up the steps and yelled through the screen door for Danielle to come out. She didn't want to track dirt into her grandma's house, nor did she want to take off her sneakers just to put them right back on.

Grandma Annie came to the front door and asked, "Child, why is you out here yelling instead of coming inside to get your sister?" Then she saw Laura! "Oh my, I see why you didn't come inside!" she said with love and laughter in her voice. Stepping out on to the porch wearing a flowery, oversized cotton shift dress and house shoes, Grandma Annie continued, "I guess I don't need to ask how was your first day on the tobacco farm."

"Oh, Grandma, it was nonstop; we stood up all day, and that tobacco was wet and dirty," Laura explained while taking a seat on the top porch step.

But she was quick to add that everybody was really nice to them. She didn't want her grandma thinking the work was too hard and telling her mama that she shouldn't go back out to the tobacco farm. Laura continued telling her grandma about the three older women working with them and showing them what to do with the loose tobacco. After updating her grandma, Laura was ready to go home and take a shower.

"Where's Danielle?" she inquired.

Her lil sis was inside looking at the cartoons but came outside when she heard Laura call her name. Danielle started laughing and giggling when she saw Laura. The dried dirt on Laura's forehead, arms, and legs really tickled her lil sis.

"Don't laugh at your sister," Grandma Annie admonished Danielle. "But she does look a mess," she teased with a smile and wink over the top of her glasses at the little girl.

"Ugh, come on, Danielle, bye Grandma, see you tomorrow," Laura said all in one breath while walking back down the steps. It was hot, and Laura was ready to go; she knew they still had to walk a couple of streets over to get home. She fast walked Danielle the two streets over to their house. Laura left her dirty, wet, and smelly sneakers on the front porch.

Laura turned the television on *Scooby-Doo* cartoons for Danielle then headed straight for the bathroom. She took off those filthy clothes and took a nice long shower. The warm water felt so good that she didn't want to come out of the shower. Laura finally came out of the bathroom carrying a plastic bag. She had taken the plastic trash bag out of the trashcan in the bathroom and put her dirty clothes into it. She knew her mama would have a fit if she put those filthy work clothes in the hamper with the regular dirty clothes.

It was already almost 7:30 p.m. and would still be light for another hour or so, but Laura put on her pajamas anyway. She was tired and ready for bed but went down the small hallway to the kitchen. Laura took the chicken, rice, and string beans from Sunday's dinner out of the refrigerator. She dished out food for her and Danielle and put it in the oven. Laura saw that her mama had also prepared a spaghetti casserole, so she knew what dinner would be for the next couple of days. The two girls watched an episode of *Scooby-Doo* while eating their dinner.

Danielle was still underfoot as Laura put the dishes away and headed to their bedroom to figure out what to wear to the tobacco farm tomorrow. Maybe Aunt Nicky's old clothes can finally be used for something useful, Laura thought as she put a pile of them in the center of her bed.

"Why were you so dirty when you came home?" Danielle asked.

Laura explained to the little chatter box that it was because they were working on a farm hanging wet tobacco on sticks all day.

"So, you were hanging cigarettes on sticks," Danielle responded with a confused look on her face.

Laura could not help but fall onto the bed laughing. She explained to her lil sis that it is the tobacco before it's made into cigarettes. Laura knew that cigarettes, cigars, and snuff came from tobacco, but she had to admit that prior to today, she didn't know those items came from those huge green leaves they strung all day.

She had seen Grandma Annie occasionally dip Tube Rose snuff, and her mama sometimes smoked cigarettes.

Looking through the clothes, Laura found a few pair of jeans that fit her big and baggy. She decided that she could roll up the pant legs and wear a belt. There were also a few large long-sleeve button-down cotton blouses. Laura took out one of her own dark tank shirts to wear under the button-down blouse. Mrs. Cindy's son Daniel, with the nice smile, crossed her mind as she laid out the clothes. Laura thought to herself, I don't want to look too unkept tomorrow. So even though Laura knew that she would get wet and dirty, she decided to press the clothes anyway because they had been balled up in a pile on the floor of the closet she shared with Danielle.

After filling the bathtub for Danielle, she sat down on the bed to call Sydney. "Hey girl, what are you doing?" Laura greeted her best friend.

"Can you believe it's just now getting dark outside, and I'm already in my pajamas ready to go to bed?" Sydney responded.

"Yeah," Laura said, "that's the most standing with outstretched arms I have ever done at one time. Those women's hands were moving like lightning."

"I know," Sydney responded. "Jacob hasn't come out of his room since dinner; I think he's asleep already. You know he's still trying to play recreational league baseball this summer." Sydney then asked Laura, "What are you wearing tomorrow?"

"I went through some of my Aunt Nicky's old clothes and picked out a pair of jeans and a top. They are a little big but will work for the tobacco farm. I don't want to look too crazy," Laura added. Both girls broke out into giggles.

"I'm going to wear jeans, and I'm going ask Jacob or my dad if I can wear one of their old shirts," said Sydney.

"Cool, let me go and get Danielle out of this tub; I'll see you in the morning," Laura responded. As Laura was hanging up the phone, she heard her brother, John, coming in the door. He must have gotten off from work early. She yelled toward the bathroom for Danielle to get out of the tub and walked down the little hallway to put the phone back on the side table in the living room. Their phone had an extra-long cord that reached throughout the whole house; you could even take it out onto the front porch to talk.

Laura gave John a rundown of her first day on the tobacco farm. He settled on to the couch and started flipping channels until he reached the baseball game. For a minute, she thought he wasn't really listening to her until he commented that it would all be worth it, come Friday, her first payday. Yes, and in cash, Laura thought as she went back to her bedroom.

Danielle already had on her pajamas and was insistent that Laura read her a story. OK, what shall we read tonight, Laura mused as she climbed into bed with her little sister and picked up a book from the small bedside table that separated the two twin beds. Ah, let's finish the princess book, and that's the last thing Laura remembered because when she woke up, it was pitch-black dark and Danielle was sound asleep. She glanced at the clock, and it was almost midnight. Her mama would be getting off soon. Laura eased out of the bed, not wanting to wake Danielle. She set the alarm for 6:00 a.m. and got into her own twin bed, falling right back to sleep.

It seemed like Laura had just settled into her own bed when the blare of the alarm clock startled her awake. It was Tuesday, workday two on the tobacco farm. She quickly turned the alarm off and then just laid there for a minute before going to the bathroom. Laura put her hair up into a fresh ponytail but added a navy-blue polyester headband to catch some of the sweat that she knew would be rolling down her face. Laura took a quick peep into her mama's room, and she was sound asleep.

Dropping two slices of bread into the toaster, it hit her. Laura was too tired and the evening went by so fast yesterday that she had forgotten all about fixing a lunch for today. She opened the refrigerator and didn't see anything that would hold up in the heat. She didn't have a mini cooler or insulated lunch box, so Laura surveyed the kitchen and took two apples, put some dry cereal into a plastic sandwich bag, and took two of the little juice boxes from the refrigerator. She put everything into a paper bag.

Laura sat at the table eating her toast. She pondered asking John to pick her up some lunch stuff from the grocery store. That was going to be another deduction from her $200 pay on Friday. Laura quietly left the house, making sure the front door was locked behind her.

Laura saw the crew as she turned the corner and walked toward Sydney's house. It was just about 6:50 a.m. Laura noticed that everybody had on a pair of regular blue jeans today. Sydney and Amy also had on oversized button-down shirts. The guys had on short-sleeve t-shirts again, but today they were black. As they were laughing and talking, Mr. Isaiah and Mr. Nate pulled up at precisely 7:00 a.m.

He greeted the teens with his bellowing voice, and Mr. Nate gave them all a good morning nod of his head. While they were climbing into the cargo bed of the truck, Mr. Wilson shouted morning from the porch and reminded them not to forget their lunches. There were four school lunch boxes sitting on the little table on the porch. A couple of them were covered in cartoons. Must be their little brother's or sister's, Laura thought. She guessed she could have used Danielle's lunch box; it was covered in *Scooby-Doo* cartoons. Mike and Amy picked up the cartoon lunch boxes. Oh well Laura sighed the lunch bag will have to do for today.

Laura remembered the route from yesterday. The breeze flowing into the truck made for limited conversation, and she assessed from the quietness that everybody was probably still a little tired from their first day on the tobacco farm. Laura's thoughts went to the waiting truckload of tobacco. She hoped that if her, Sydney, and Amy got a faster rhythm going maybe they could at least get a few extra minutes break between truckload swap outs. No way we're going to get as fast as Mrs. Mary and the women, she mused, but maybe just a little faster.

"OK, girls, see you around lunchtime," Mr. Isaiah shouted from the truck cab. He didn't get out of the truck this morning because he had already introduced the three girls to the three women yesterday. After they jumped out the back of the truck, Jacob handed two lunch boxes to his sister, Sydney. Mike handed his lunch box to Amy. Mrs. Mary came walking toward them.

"Good morning, Mary," Mr. Isaiah shouted.

That loud, bellowing voice must be Mr. Isaiah's natural voice because he's so tall and big, Laura surmised. The girls had heard Mr. Nate talk yesterday when he did the truck swap outs, and he was not nearly as loud as his cousin, Mr. Isaiah.

"Good morning, fellas. You girls all ready for day two?" Mrs. Mary greeted them.

"Yes, ma'am," they said in unison as they waved at Jacob and Mike, then turned to walk toward the barn overhang.

The girls put the lunches on the long table that was up against the barn wall under the overhang with the water Igloo and the three coolers. They got into their same positions as yesterday. Laura and Sydney on either side of Mrs. Mary and Amy in between Mrs. Cindy and Miss Elaine.

"Let's get to it!" Mrs. Mary said. "This truckload of tobacco ain't going to string itself."

Laura noticed that all the full sticks from yesterday were gone and about half of this truck was already bundled. What time did they start, she wondered...must be right at sunup. The girls grabbed a stick with string and started grabbing batches of tobacco leaves for bundling. They started very slow, but their rhythm started to pick up toward the end of the first truckload.

The morning was passing swiftly; they were on the third truck already, signaling that it was almost time for their lunch break. The older women were stringing and talking without even looking down. It was like their hands knew when they had about fifteen leaves. Mrs. Mary and Mrs. Cindy were talking about how their husbands and sons were meat-and-potatoes people. They wanted a full meal after working in the tobacco field all day. Laura learned that the women did a lot of prep cooking of various meats, like fried chicken, meat loaf, and roasts, over the weekend, then only had to cook some rice or boil potatoes and vegetables in the evening. It sounded like a lot of the vegetables came from their own gardens. Her mama usually cooked a one-pot casserole dish on Mondays and another one on Thursdays, but she did fry up some delicious chicken to carry over to Grandma Annie's on Sundays.

Like clockwork, around 12:15 p.m. they saw the two trucks turning off the road onto the dirt road leading up to the barn. Laura learned from yesterday's drive to Walker's Country Store that most of those side roads they saw when driving out to the tobacco farm lead somewhere, whether to a store, another farm, or maybe even a neighborhood. She quickly looked down at her clothes as the trucks approached. Her shirt and jeans were still pretty dirty, but at least her arms and legs were covered up and not as wet. She glanced at Sydney and Amy, and they looked about the same as her. She could feel the wet headband from the sweat but didn't want to reach up and touch it to get dirt on her forehead.

Jacob and Mike had already told Mr. Isaiah that they were staying at the tobacco barn for lunch. Laura was hungry, especially after listening to the women talk about all the food they cooked up for the week. She really wasn't looking forward to just having two apples and some dry cereal.

Mr. Roy Smith and Anthony walked up and greeted Mrs. Mary. Anthony continued to the back of the overhang and picked up one of the coolers. Mr. David Ingram and his sons, David Jr. and Daniel, greeted Mrs. Cindy. The brothers also picked up their family cooler. Everybody was busy getting their lunch containers. Laura noticed that all the guys' hands and arms were clean. They must have washed up at a field outhouse or somewhere before coming to the barn. The men took some folding chairs from inside the barn door out to one of the big trees while the women took a quick outhouse break to wash their hands.

Laura wasn't quite sure what to do; she really didn't want to sit on the ground under a tree. There were clearly only six folding chairs for the adults. The three teen country boys came from the adult tree with what looked like full plates of food.

David Jr. spoke up and said, "We usually just sit in the bed of the truck y'all done emptied and eat our lunch."

So, the five guys—Jacob, Mike, Anthony, David Jr., and Daniel—jumped into the bed of the truck. They were all wearing ball caps because there was not a drop of shade covering the back of that truck.

Sydney said to Laura and Amy, "Let's sit up on the worktable, at least it's under the overhang and out of the direct sun."

From where Laura sat, she got a good view of Daniel. The guys were eating and talking about sports. Softball seemed to be the topic of the day. Laura was intently listening to the guys' conversation, trying to pick up the distinctiveness of Daniel's voice among the five teen boys. Glancing at him while eating her apple, she observed that his face and arms were evenly tanned with a cocoa-brown hue, and when he laughed dimples popped out around his cheekbones. He looked as if the sun had bent down and given him a perfect kiss. Oh, where did that thought come from, Laura mused.

"Is that all you're going to eat?" Sydney asked, bringing Laura out of her thoughts on Daniel's appearance.

"Girl, last night I was so tired I completely forgot to fix some lunch," she replied to Sydney.

"Do you want half of my sandwich? It's PB&J," Sydney offered.

"No, thanks, I'm good," Laura responded and bit into her apple.

"We may have to get us some mini-Igloos like Mr. Isaiah and Mr. Nate to keep our food cool," Amy chimed in. "I wanted to bring a lunch meat sandwich but didn't think it would survive in this heat."

It turned out that Amy, Sydney, Mike, and Jacob all had a PB&J sandwich, bag of chips, and an apple. Apples were the fruit of the day. Laura knew they would have to figure out how to bring a better lunch.

"All right, young people, let's get moving; it'll be time to head back out to the tobacco field in a few minutes," Mr. Roy Smith shouted out as he brought his family cooler and placed it on the back table. The others followed suit, bringing the coolers and the folding chairs. They seemed to work in harmony and had everything timed just right because sure enough, right at 1:00 p.m. came Mr. Isaiah and Mr. Nate rolling down the dirt road. They switched out the trucks, and the guys loaded up. Both trucks went clickety-clanking back up the dirt road. The women and girls took their positions and got busy stringing the fourth truck. As they started back to work, Laura thought to herself that it might not have been too bad to sit under one of the trees during lunch to catch some fresh air and maybe a little breeze.

By the time they started working on the fifth and final truck of the day, Laura asked, "What time do y'all start working in the mornings, because the first truck is about halfway done when we get here?"

Miss Elaine spoke up, explaining that she rides in with Cindy and her family. She only lives about a mile from them. Mrs. Cindy chimed in, also explaining that her husband Roy drops them off about 6:30 a.m. before heading out to the tobacco fields. She also teased Miss Elaine about Mr. Kevin riding in with them so he could see his sweetie for a few minutes before starting work. The women burst into laughter at their light bantering.

Mrs. Mary continued, explaining that her family also got there around the same time. Mr. Nate Thompson picked them up in the mornings because they only lived about a mile or so from him in the direction of the tobacco farm. All the ladies agreed that the driving arrangement helped to keep from having too many empty trucks parked out by the fields because there were a few other workers that also drove in.

All of them seemed to live at least a mile apart, which seemed like pretty far apart to Laura. She could walk to Grandma Annie's or Sydney's house in less than five minutes. Laura's legs were starting to feel like she had been standing forever, and her arms seemed to be in a permanent outstretched position as she bundled and hung the last bit of tobacco in truck five. She couldn't imagine having to walk a mile to Grandma Annie's house to get her lil sis after working all day stringing tobacco. Looking across the table at Amy, she saw that the oversized shirts were definitely helping to keep them dry, but the front of their shirts were still pretty dirty. She looked over at Miss Elaine and Mrs. Cindy, and they didn't seem to be getting as dirty. Laura thought there must be something to this technique that she and the girls had not figured out yet. By the end of the week, Laura would realize that because the girls were shorter, smaller, and arms not as long as the adult women, the tobacco leaves were rubbing much closer up against their bodies every time they strung and looped a bundle.

Finally, the three trucks were coming down the drive, signaling the end of the workday. They had just finished the last few bundles. As Mr. Nate was switching out the trucks and getting everything set for Wednesday morning, the young people congregated at the back table to gather their lunch containers. Laura had thrown her paper bag away, so she was just standing by the worktable waiting to load up in the truck.

Standing not too far from Laura, Daniel asked, "How do you like working out here so far?"

"It's not too bad, just hot," Laura responded.

Before Daniel could respond, his brother, David Jr., walked up with the family cooler and announced that it was time to go. Everybody was ready to go as they jumped into the various trucks. By the time the truck pulled up in front of Sydney's house, Jacob and Mike were asleep again.

Laura whispered to Sydney, "The breeze flowing into the back of the truck must be putting them to sleep after working in the tobacco field all day."

Mrs. Wilson was already outside sitting on the porch. She stood up and walked to the top step. She and Mr. Isaiah greeted each other with him never turning off the truck. Jumping out the back of the truck, Laura pulled out her watch, and it was 6:03 p.m. The man was punctual.

While saying her goodbyes to everyone, Laura unbuttoned her oversized blouse and took it off. At least she wouldn't look too dirty walking to Grandma Annie's and then home. Mike waited for Amy, and they turned to walk up the street together.

Grandma Annie was sitting on the porch waiting for Laura. "Well, you don't look quite as dirty as yesterday, but you moving kinda slow," her grandma greeted Laura.

"Grandma, I feel like my legs and arms are gonna fall off, and it's so hot," Laura slightly whined, not wanting her grandma to be too concerned.

"Ain't no big fans in that barn?" her grandma asked.

"No, ma'am, and we work right outside the barn under this big overhang. A big fan would probably blow that tobacco all over the place," Laura explained.

They both had a good laugh at the thought of that sight with tobacco leaves flying everywhere!

"Grandma, do you have anything that I can take for lunch tomorrow?" Laura asked.

"Let me see what I can get for you while I pry your sister from these afternoon cartoons," Grandma Annie responded while getting up and going into the house.

Laura had been standing at the bottom of the steps, so she walked up and sat in one of the porch chairs. Aw that feels good, she thought as she leaned back. Laura was tired and it seemed like she had only been sitting there for a minute when her grandma was back on the porch with a brown paper lunch bag. Danielle was right behind her. Bouncing out the front door, all bubbly and happy as usual.

Laura fast walked her lil sis to their house. She wasn't quite as dirty as yesterday but still didn't want to run into any of her friends. Danielle had eaten dinner at Grandma Annie's, so Laura just dished out a little of the spaghetti casserole and put it in a smaller dish to warm in the oven. There was a note from her mama taped to the refrigerator. It read: You were asleep when I came in from work last night, and I was asleep when you left for work this morning. I hope your couple of days on the tobacco farm have gone well. What are you carrying for lunch...cereal...the box was on the counter. There is some PB&J and cookies in the cupboard, and I bought some bananas and apples today. Mama.

Now, what exactly did Grandma Annie give me for lunch? Laura pondered as she put the note down and picked up the brown paper bag from the counter. Oh my gosh, she laughed, the bag contained two PB&J sandwiches, two bags of chips, two packages of crackers, an apple, and a banana. Well at least it was enough for Wednesday and Thursday.

After showering, Laura decided to go ahead and fix Danielle's bath so she could have a quiet minute to eat while her lil sis bathed. After finishing her spaghetti, she called Sydney to chat about their first couple of days working. They really didn't have as much time to talk throughout the day as they initially thought they would have. Danielle came running down the hallway and jumped on the couch beside Laura.

"Girl, I've got to go. I'll see you in the morning; remember to bring a towel so we can sit under the tree for lunch," Laura reminded Sydney.

"OK, I'll call Amy and tell her too," Sydney said before hanging up.

As Laura put the phone back on the side table, the girls heard the door lock turn and in walked their brother, John.

"Hey, lil bit, here, I bought you something from the grocery store," he said while handing Danielle a pack of Now and Later candy.

"Oh no," Laura spoke up. "Not this late. I already gave her a couple of cookies and juice earlier for snack. Put those up for tomorrow," she directed to Danielle.

"Hey, sis, I got a pack for you too." And John handed a pack to Laura.

"Thanks, I'll take mine for lunch tomorrow."

Danielle continued to hold on tightly to her candy. They both laughed at her. John didn't have to go into the grocery store until around midday, so he got to spend some daylight hours with Danielle and Mama. Their mama usually didn't get up until around 9:00 or 10:00 a.m.

Danielle put her candy on the shared night table between their twin beds as she got into her bed.

"OK, where did we stop?" Laura asked as they snuggled into her lil sis's bed.

"Page three," Danielle laughed.

According to the clock, it was a little after 11:00 p.m. when Laura woke up and got into her own bed. At this rate it was going to take all summer to finish reading that one princess story.

Wednesday morning at 6:00 a.m. came early.

The morning seemed to go by pretty fast. Maybe because it was midweek or the girls were getting used to the continuous rotation of tobacco trucks. It was already lunchtime, which meant the young teen crew had officially made it halfway through their first week. Two-and-a-half days to go, Laura smiled inside as everybody grabbed their lunch containers. All three of the girls had brought a large towel with them. They had already told Jacob and Mike on the morning drive out to the farm that they planned to sit under one of the shade trees and eat lunch.

Evidently the guys must have told Anthony, David Jr., and Daniel because everybody walked out to the trees. They all sat in a semicircle under a tree not too far from where the adults were having their lunch. The tree was large with huge shade branches, but some of the guys were still partly in the sun. They didn't seem to mind as the conversation flowed. The guys joked with the girls about their towels; it wasn't as if their jeans were not already dirty. Laura and the girls had not thought about that aspect. Everybody had a good laugh.

During the teens' lunch conversation, Laura learned that David Jr. played football while Daniel played softball and basketball. Anthony also played softball and basketball. They both were playing on a summer recreational league team like Jacob and Mike. Where in the world did they get the time and energy after all day in that hot tobacco field? Laura wondered. Sydney had told her that Jacob and Mike had missed practice, but the coach still let them be on the team.

"Amy and Mike seem to be having a little one-on-one conversation," Laura whispered to Sydney.

Laura didn't dare say anything directly to Daniel. She didn't want to bring any attention to herself. Everybody saw the black truck coming down the dirt road and knew it was time to start the second half of the workday. Laura didn't even have to look at her watch because she knew it was around 1:05 p.m.

After lunch on Wednesday, the rest of the week flew by. It was the end of the workday on Thursday, and Laura was in her own little world during the ride home. She was ruminating over what happened during lunch. Sydney had sat to her right and then Daniel sat down right beside her on the left. Anthony sat on the other side of him. Daniel and Anthony mainly talked about the upcoming Saturday softball games. Daniel had turned slightly toward Laura and asked about her lunch and if she was OK. He must have noticed that she only ate half of her PB&J sandwich. She had smiled and said it was fine. Laura was tired of PB&J. Well make sure you drink plenty of water to stay hydrated, Daniel had told her, flashing that megawatt smile. Obviously, he thought nothing of using the outhouse, Laura laughed to herself.

"Hey girl," Sydney said, bringing Laura back to the present. "Tomorrow is our first cash payday!"

"Yes!" Laura declared. "And I am ready!"

The girls had already made plans to go to the City Center Mall. It was still fairly new, having been opened for only about five years. There were a few stores still downtown on Main Street, but most of the teens either took the bus or got dropped off at the mall for a few hours. The mall food court had quickly become the Saturday spot among the youth in Ervinsville. They had done nothing the whole week but string tobacco and sleep. The teen girls were ready to wear some regular clothes and have some fun. Both girls were laughing and talking about their Saturday plans as Mr. Isaiah pulled up in front of Sydney's house.

Mrs. Wilson was waiting on the front porch. "Hey Isaiah, I missed you at Bible study last night," she said from the top step as they all jumped out of the back of the truck.

"Yeah, I told Dorothy to go on without me; we had some rotating to do out on the farm."

"OK, take care," Mrs. Wilson responded.

Laura wondered how Mr. Isaiah and his family came to attend Sydney's church instead of going to a church in their community out in the country. She would have to ask Sydney.

Laura was joyfully thinking about tomorrow's payday as she walked down the street toward Grandma Annie's house. All kinds of shopping thoughts were twirling in her head. She had never had her own money to spend, except maybe $20 of birthday money. She quickly gathered up Danielle and started the walk home.

They were almost home when Laura spotted a couple of neighborhood girls and Eric walking toward them. Suddenly, Laura became very self-conscious of how she looked in the baggy, dirty jeans, even though she had taken off and was carrying the dirty blouse.

She could feel the damp headband; her face felt sticky and dirty from sweating all day.

"Hey, Laura, what are you up to?" Carolyn greeted her.

"Nothing much, we're on our way home from my grandma's house," Laura responded.

"Yeah, we heard that you, Sydney, and Amy were working out on a farm this summer," Brenda added.

"Yep, they make tobacco cigarettes!" Danielle shouted out.

Carolyn and Brenda burst into laughter and said almost simultaneously, "You sure do look like a farm girl."

"We got part-time jobs in K's, the new teen clothing store in the mall; we only work about four or five hours a few days a week," Carolyn announced with a smirky smile.

Eric quickly interjected, "Hey, we're on our way to the school ballfield to play a game of pickup softball; do you want to come up and watch or play?"

Laura grabbed her lil sister's hand and replied, "No, not today."

She continued walking toward home as the three teens continued toward the ballfield. As they turned down their street, Laura was quiet; a sudden weightiness came over her. Danielle sensed it.

Her lil sis pensively said, "Laura, I'm sorry about telling them you make tobacco cigarettes on the farm."

"It's OK," Laura assured Danielle as she knelt down and hugged her. "Let's go watch some *Scooby-Doo*!"

After finally getting Danielle settled into bed, Laura called Sydney. She told Sydney about her encounter with Eric, Carolyn, and Brenda. The two girls were so annoying to Laura, especially bragging about their summer part-time jobs at the mall.

"Girl, don't pay them any attention because I'm sure we're making more money than they are." Sydney continued, "I think Eric works in a sneaker store because I heard him talking to Jacob on the porch. They play on the same softball team. You know Carolyn is a senior and Brenda and Eric are juniors, so we probably won't see too much of them at the high school."

"Thank goodness," Laura responded. "I'll see you tomorrow."

"OK, cause tomorrow can't come soon enough," Sydney said.

"Payday!" They both exclaimed at the same time while hanging up with laughter in the air. Laura always felt better after talking and laughing with Sydney.

Friday, their first payday! Laura was wide awake, and it wasn't even 6:00 a.m. yet; the clock was showing 5:34 a.m. She had barely slept all night thinking about getting paid today. Laura turned off the alarm clock and got up. While eating her toast and sipping on a glass of juice, she remembered that she had to give her mama a portion of her pay. Laura couldn't recall her mama telling her a specific amount; well, it can't be too much, maybe $20. She also wanted to buy a small insulated lunch box over the weekend so that she could take something other than PB&J sandwiches for lunch for the next five weeks on the tobacco farm.

Laura was not the only one who couldn't sleep. As she approached Sydney's house a little early, everyone was already on the porch. The atmosphere was happy and upbeat. Everybody was talking about getting paid and weekend plans. Mr. Isaiah and Mr. Nate pulled up at precisely 7:00 a.m. Boy, they must have an inner clock, Laura thought, because every morning this week they were right on time.

Mr. Wilson came out on to the porch and said, "Good morning, Isaiah, these young folks are super excited today about their first payday."

"Morning, I'm sure they are," Mr. Isaiah bellowed back.

All three men good-heartedly laughed as the young crew got into the back of the truck. During the drive out to the tobacco farm, Laura's thoughts returned to their new friends, Daniel, David Jr., and Anthony, but especially Daniel. She wondered what plans they had for the weekend. She already knew Daniel and Anthony had softball games on Saturday morning. Maybe they were planning to come into the city and go to the mall; it was only thirty miles. She looked around the truck. Jacob and Mike were leaning back, enjoying the morning breeze. Sydney was talking to Amy.

Laura said to both of them, "I sure hope today goes by fast. I wonder what Mrs. Mary and them have planned for the weekend."

"Hum, I'm sure they'll be talking about it this morning," Sydney said as the truck turned down the now very familiar dirt road.

"See y'all around noon," Mr. Isaiah shouted as the girls jumped out of the back of the truck.

Mrs. Mary greeted the girls and waved at the guys as Mr. Isaiah turned the truck around in one swift move and was gone back up the dirt road. As usual the three women had already put a good dent into stringing and bundling the first truckload of tobacco. They were stringing and talking about their weekend plans. Laura and Sydney peeped at each other around Mrs. Mary and smiled. Laura was still amazed at how the women could carry on a full conversation without slowing their rhythm down at all. If she got too engrossed listening to the talk, her hands always slowed down, and it's not as if she was stringing that fast to start with.

From the conversation it appeared the women had a lot of housework to do over the weekend. There was talk about working in their gardens, cleaning the house, and doing laundry. Also cooking for a family cookout on Sunday after church. None of that sounded like fun to Laura after a week working in tobacco, except maybe the cookout. She knew the women were probably around the same age as her mama, except maybe Miss Elaine. Laura didn't hear any mention of the boys and their weekend plans. Maybe over lunch, she thought as she tried to string a little faster.

Their lunch break could not have come soon enough; they were finally finishing up the third truck when Laura heard the two trucks coming down the rocky dirt road. It was a beautiful sunny day, and she was looking forward to sitting under the large shade tree for a few minutes. The guys jumped out of the back of the truck and greeted everyone while heading toward the barn to get the folding chairs and lunch coolers. Everybody moved quickly to get set up under the trees; they wanted to take full advantage of their lunch break.

This time instead of driving right back off, Mr. Isaiah and Mr. Nate got out of the truck and lifted a large cooler from out of the back of the cargo bed and carried it out to the shade trees.

"My watermelons are coming in pretty good this year," Mr. Isaiah announced. "Dorothy cut up a couple of them last night and put them in the fridge so they would be nice and cold today. There're slices on ice in this cooler for y'all to enjoy."

"Oh, that sounds good! Be sure and tell Dorothy we said thank you," Mrs. Mary announced for the group.

"Sure will, see you all in a few," Mr. Isaiah shouted as he and Mr. Nate turned to leave for their lunch break.

The adults settled under their tree, and the young folks under the teen lunch tree, which was about a stone's throw away from the adults.

Laura asked Sydney, "Why does Mr. Isaiah and his family come into the city to go to your church?"

"Mrs. Dorothy's family has been members of our church for years; after they got married, he started coming also. I don't know exactly how they met," Sydney explained.

"Oh, OK, I was just wondering since Mrs. Mary and them all seem to be connected to the community out here," Laura responded.

"You know, my mom's family lived in the country a long time ago when she was a little girl; that's how she knows about tobacco," Sydney added.

Grandma Annie had never mentioned living in the country; as far as Laura knew they had always lived in Ervinsville. The watermelon slices were sweet and cold. Laura ate two of them. She didn't want to look greedy and also didn't want to have to go back and forth to that outhouse all afternoon. The guys ate a whole lot more watermelon; they said the slices were small. Daniel had sat beside her again. He and Anthony seemed pretty hyped up about their softball game on Saturday.

"That was really nice of Mr. Isaiah," Laura said directly to Daniel as they all started to get up and clean the lunch area.

"Yeah, that watermelon hit the spot," Daniel said as he stretched out his hand toward Laura to help her get up off the grass.

Laura missed his gesture and was already getting up with her PB&J sandwich balled up in her bag. She was glad today was Friday for more than one reason. Everybody was ready to get the second half of the day over, get paid, and start the weekend.

"What are you girls going to do this weekend with your first paychecks?" Mrs. Mary asked as they started work on the fourth truck.

"Well," Laura spoke up, "we've been out of school for three weeks and haven't done anything fun. We're going to the mall to do a little shopping and browsing. The mall also has a food court where we can meet up with some friends."

Amy chimed in. "There are a couple of nice stores downtown on Main Street also that I want to check out, like the Kress store and Roses."

Laura thought to herself, I have enough of Aunt Nicky's old Kress clothes, I'm wearing them right now.

"Well, I hope you girls don't spend all your money this weekend and put a little to the side," Mrs. Cindy advised. She continued, "Our boys must save some of their money so they can have funds for school activities and such throughout the school year."

"Yes, these children can keep your pockets empty," Mrs. Mary added.

All the women laughed, including Miss Elaine. I wonder if she has any little children at home, Laura mused to herself. The afternoon zipped by; they were finishing up the last few tobacco leaves in the fifth truck when the three trucks came rolling down the road.

Mr. Isaiah walked toward the barn with some white envelopes in his hand.

"Thank you, girls, for hanging in here this week; I hope you plan to come back next week," Mr. Isaiah said as he handed each of them a white envelope with their name written on it.

"Yes, sir!" they all said in unison.

"OK, let's load up and get y'all home for the weekend," he bellowed.

Everybody was shouting out goodbyes and have a good weekend when Daniel said "See you on Monday" to Laura as he walked past her carrying his family's cooler.

"OK, I hope y'all win on Saturday!" Laura shouted back.

The city teen crew climbed in the back of the truck, waving at their newfound friends as Mr. Isaiah turned the truck around to take them home for the weekend. Laura had folded her envelope in half and safely tucked it into her pocket. The jeans pocket was deep, so there was no chance of it falling out. She wasn't about to take her envelope out in the back of the truck and let the wind possibly take it away. She laughed at the thought and knew she would probably jump out the back of that truck after her envelope! Jacob and Mike were not sleeping today; they were talking about their softball game tomorrow and whether the coach would let them play. Amy had plans to take her two little brothers down to the ballpark to watch the softball game. Laura and Sydney gave each other the eye and giggled, knowing Amy was more interested in Mike than softball.

Mrs. Wilson was on duty, waiting for them on the porch. "Evening Isaiah, I see everybody worked a full week," she greeted them.

"Yes, and they did a fine job; these some hardworking young folks. Y'all get some rest, enjoy your weekend, and I'll see you 7:00 a.m. Monday morning," Mr. Isaiah responded. "See y'all on Sunday," he directed to Mrs. Wilson and then sped off down the street.

"Well, young folks, how does it feel to get that first paycheck?" Mrs. Wilson inquired.

"Great!" they responded with full smiles as each one subconsciously touched their pants pocket.

"Well don't spend it all in one weekend, put a little to the side. These two here already know," Mrs. Wilson said as she pointed to Jacob and Sydney with a motherly wink.

"Yep," Jacob responded as he headed into the house, no doubt to beat Sydney to the shower.

That was the second time today adults had given them the exact same advice about not spending all of their money and saving. Mike and Amy turned and walked toward their houses.

"Girl, I'm just focusing on working, getting paid, and shopping," Laura said in low voice to Sydney on the sidewalk out of Mrs. Wilson's earshot from the top of the porch, or at least she hoped it was out of earshot.

"And I saw Daniel talking to you today," Sydney said with a grin.

"Girl, please," Laura laughed. "I'll come to your house tomorrow around 10:30 a.m. so we can walk to the bus stop to catch the 11:00 a.m. bus downtown then the transfer bus to the mall."

Solidifying their Saturday plans, Sydney walked up the steps and Laura turned to walk toward her Grandma Annie's house.

Laura was so happy that she didn't care who saw her in the dirty tobacco work clothes. Opening the front screen door, Laura shouted gleefully inside, "Grandma, I got my first pay!"

"That's great, baby," Grandma Annie said, coming to the front door. She continued, "Danielle's in the backyard playing with your Uncle Richard's girls. I'm watching them for him for a few hours."

"OK, I'll walk around back," Laura responded. Grandma Annie had a big backyard that was lined with lots of pine cone trees.

"Hey, girls; come on, Danielle, it's time to go home," Laura greeted her cousins and instructed Danielle.

"Can I just stay and play a little while longer?" Danielle whined.

"No, not today," Laura said firmly. There was no way she was walking home then walking back over here to get her lil sister.

Danielle made no movement to stop running around the backyard. Grandma Annie had walked through the house and was watching from the back screen door.

"Danielle Marie, you heard your sister!" she shouted from the door. "Come on in here, you can play with your cousins again another day."

Laura knew that when Grandma used your first and middle name, she was serious. Danielle knew it too, because she stopped running and went up the back steps into the kitchen.

"Bye, girls," Laura said to her cousins and then walked back around the house to the front porch. Danielle and Grandma Annie came out onto the front porch.

"OK, baby, I'll see y'all on Sunday. Don't spend all your money in one day; remember to put a little aside," Grandma Annie instructed Laura. Everybody was telling her to save, save, save, and all she wanted to do was shop, shop, shop.

After getting Danielle settled in front of the television watching *Scooby-Doo,* Laura went into the bedroom and took her envelope out of her jeans pocket. She counted out eight twenty-dollar bills and four ten-dollar bills—exactly $200. Laura was giddy with excitement; she counted it multiple times knowing full well that Mr. Isaiah, with his clockwork precision, had counted their money out right before giving it to them. She put her money back into the envelope and placed it under some clothes in the top chest of drawers. She shared the chest with Danielle; the top three drawers were hers and the bottom two were for her lil sister. Laura stood there for a minute. Finally her own spending money, she breathed out a sigh of relief.

Laura had dozed off to sleep, but the sound of the front door opening awakened her even though she was bone tired. She glanced at the clock, and it was almost 10:00 p.m.; must be John, she thought. She got up and walked down the hallway toward the living room.

"Hey, John, you work late tonight?" she greeted her brother.

"No, I just hung out for a couple of hours with some friends. So, you finished your first week on the tobacco farm and got paid today," he continued.

"Yes, and I can't wait to go to the mall tomorrow."

John laughed. "Girl, money goes quick; don't spend it all in one place." He settled on to the couch and began flipping channels.

Not again with the saving, Laura thought as she went back to bed.

FIRST PAYDAY WEEKEND

No alarm clock—Laura had decided to wake up naturally. She opened her eyes and glanced at the clock. It was only 7:33 a.m.; she thought that she would have at least slept until 8:00 a.m. The sun was bright and shining through the window curtains as she stretched, looking forward to the day. Laura wanted to get her work clothes washed and hung out early. They had a washing machine but no dryer. Two long clothes lines in the backyard were for hanging clothes out to dry. Danielle wasn't awake yet, but Laura knew her lil sis would be up and underfoot any minute. She grabbed the trash bag of dirty work clothes from behind the door and went into the kitchen. The washing machine was in the far corner against the backdoor wall. After putting the clothes into the wash, she went to change clothes.

"Hey, Laura, what are we doing today?" Danielle asked as she sat up in her bed.

"I'm sure Mama got something for you to do because I'm going to the mall with Sydney," Laura informed the lil girl.

"But I want to go with you," Danielle insisted to her big sister, with her voice getting louder.

Not wanting to wake up their mama, Laura promised to do something with her later in the day. That promise seemed to appease the lil girl. So, Laura had her go brush her teeth and get dressed while she fixed her some breakfast.

Danielle was finishing up her Frosted Flakes as Laura was taking the first load of clothes out of the washer. "Do you want to go outside with me while I hang out these clothes?" she asked.

"Yes!" her lil sister responded happily. It didn't take too much to lift her mood.

When the girls came back inside with the empty clothes basket, their mama was up in the kitchen, standing at the counter in her big multicolored housecoat brewing a pot of coffee. It was one of those little four-cup coffee pots because no one drank coffee but Mama. It was already a little after 9:00 a.m. Laura was keeping check on the time because she had plans to meet Sydney at 10:30 a.m. Turning from the counter, their mama greeted them and inquired as to why they were outside so early in the morning.

"I was helping Laura hang up her tobacco clothes," Danielle informed her with a big smile of accomplishment.

Laura greeted her mama and explained her Saturday plans to go to the mall with Sydney. She wanted to get her chores done early. Pouring a cup of coffee, her mama reminded Laura that it was also her weekend to clean the bathroom. You have got to be kidding me, I have been working in tobacco all week, Laura responded in her head.

Still standing and taking a sip of her coffee, her mama asked, "How was your first week on the tobacco farm? Did you all get paid yesterday?"

Laura realized this was the first time she had seen or spoken to her mama since Monday morning. "It was OK," she responded.

Laura took Danielle into the living room and settled her on the couch for Saturday morning cartoons. Her mama had sat at the kitchen table and was still sipping her cup of coffee when Laura came back into the kitchen.

"We got paid in cash just like Mr. Isaiah promised. How much do I have to give you for the household bills?" Laura asked.

"Forty dollars is good, and put aside a little for later; don't spend your whole pay today at the mall," her mama instructed.

"Yes, ma'am," she responded and slowly walked down the hallway to her bedroom to get the money.

Laura had thought it would be maybe $20 but definitely not $40. Handing the two twenty-dollar bills over to her mama, Laura's brain calculated it as handing over two pairs of new jeans. At least she was able to convince her mama to let her clean the bathroom later that evening after coming back from the mall.

Her mama placed the money in her housecoat pocket and took a sip of her second cup of coffee. Getting up to get her toast, she reminded Laura to bring in her work clothes before leaving for the mall. With the July heat, clothes dried quickly, and there were more loads of clothes to be washed and hung out. The morning was moving quickly. Laura brought in her work clothes from the line and just threw them on her bed. She had less than an hour to meet Sydney. Laura took the phone off the living room table and went back to her bedroom to dial Sydney because there was no way she was going to be over there by 10:30 a.m.

Instead of catching the bus at the top of the hill, the girls decided to walk downtown to the transfer center and catch the noon bus to the mall. The girls had walked downtown plenty of times and knew it was about a thirty-minute walk. Laura changed into a nicer pair of jean shorts that came right above her knees and a dark green tank top with little flowers all over it. It was one of her favorites, she thought as she looked at her reflection in the mirror. It looked like she was wearing a flower garden. All week in the evenings after taking her shower, Laura had just put on her pajamas and called it a day. It felt good to have on regular clothes. Since they were walking, she decided to wear her white low-cut sneakers instead of sandals. Today was going to be hot, so Laura pulled her hair back into a ponytail and then added a pair of green hoop earrings. For the finishing touch, she put on a little lip gloss. Her mama didn't let her wear makeup yet, but she was OK with Laura wearing lip gloss.

"Mama, I'm leaving, I'll be back this afternoon. Bye, Danielle, I'll bring you something back," Laura yelled out. Her lil sis glanced up from watching her cartoons and gave Laura a ready grin and a wave. Thank goodness she was too engrossed in the cartoons to make a scene. Laura heard her brother, John, going down the hallway as she exited the house. I guess he doesn't have a morning softball game, Laura mused to herself as she happily walked up the street.

Laura had brought six twenty-dollar bills, totaling $120, with her and had left the four ten-dollar bills in the envelope in her top drawer. She wore her little shoulder crossbody purse with her cash inside along with her school ID and small change purse. It held a few loose coins to catch the bus. Sydney was waiting for her on the porch, and Laura was happy to hear that Mr. Wilson was going to drop them at the bus transfer station downtown. He had to run a few errands and was going in that direction. The ride to the bus transfer station was quick.

As they were exiting the car, Mr. Wilson asked, "What time do you girls plan on leaving the mall?"

"I don't know, Dad," Sydney responded.

"Well, you need to be home by at least 6:00 p.m. That is more than enough time to be at the mall," he said.

"Yes, sir," the girls responded as they turned to walk toward the waiting buses.

Finally, Laura thought, they were settled on the city bus and on their way to the mall. The bus was full, probably because it was midday on a Saturday and people were out and about. Laura recognized a few faces from the neighborhood. Her thoughts briefly drifted to Daniel and whether his team had won their morning softball game.

"What store do you want to go to first?" Sydney asked. "The bus lets us off at the food court entrance, so if you want to, we can start from there and walk all the way to the end and then back down the other side."

"OK, sounds good. I definitely want to stop in Lerner's store; they have cute clothes," Laura responded.

They exited the bus and walked toward the food court. As they started walking into the mall, the girls briefly discussed how much spending money they had brought with them. Sydney had brought $100 with her because her mom had her hold back $100 due to the good sales for school clothes not starting until August. Everything on sale now was summer clothes. Sydney's mom wanted her to start checking out the Sunday sales flyers. Laura had brought $120 with her. She didn't say anything to Sydney about having to give her mama $40. It was around noon, but the girls were too excited to even think about eating, they kept right on walking past the various food stands.

Laura was ecstatic. They had been to the mall numerous times, but mostly she just had enough money for bus fare and snacks. She and Sydney had done a lot of window shopping but not today; she was going to make some purchases. The girls strolled along, stopping to gaze at different window displays. One store's neatly stacked stone-washed jeans caught their eyes, and they went inside. The jeans were on sale for $17.99 a pair. Both girls selected two pairs, one in blue and the second pair in black. The store also carried t-shirts and other accessories, but the girls didn't want to do all their shopping in one store. With tax they spent about $38.00.

They made a stop in the sneaker store to try on a few different color high- and low-top Converse classics and some Reebok. The sneakers were kind of expensive. After trying on a few pairs, the teens decided to put the purchase off until later. They were hoping for a good back-to-school sale.

"We'll have to ask Eric about any sales because he works in here part-time," Sydney commented.

"Yeah, I don't see him in here today; maybe he had a softball game," Laura surmised.

Laura and Sydney continued their stroll, thoroughly enjoying being out and about with a few dollars to spend. Another clothing store with racks and racks of colorful tanks, t-shirts, and blouses caught their attention. They were on sale three for $9.99. Laura squealed, pulling Sydney's arm toward the store. The teens spent over thirty minutes picking out one of each type of top. They decided to get all different colors, not wanting to be twinning too much in high school.

Next stop Lerner's, they both agreed as they continued their stroll. Laura loved going into Lerner's because they had a cool fashionable teen section, even though she had never actually purchased anything from the store. Sundresses, jumpers, skirts, blouses—she was overwhelmed and wanted to try on everything. Laura did a quick check of her cash while in the dressing room, she had $71 left. She decided on one sundress that was on sale and a jumper dress that was not on sale. They fit perfect; no alterations needed. She wanted to get a blouse to go with the jumper dress but decided it could wait. The sundress was on sale for $7.50 but the jumper was $14.99. Sydney decided to get just one sundress because she wanted them to go into the accessory store at the other end of the mall that sold hundreds of earrings, bracelets, and hair accessories.

It was almost 3:00 p.m., and the girls were starting to get a little hungry, so they decided to start strolling down the opposite side of the mall in the direction of the food court.

"Oh, let's go in here!" Sydney said as they approached Claire's accessory store. "They have everything!"

Both girls' ears were pierced, and they spent nearly an hour looking at earrings up against their ears in the mirrors throughout the store. A package of ten pairs of differently styled hoops were on sale for $8.50. Both girls got a pack. Laura also got two packages of multicolored hair barrettes for Danielle. Her total purchase came up to $11 and change.

It was almost 4:00 p.m. by the time the girls got to the food court.

"We'd better catch the 4:00 p.m. bus back downtown and get something to eat on Main Street," Sydney stated, "because the next bus won't be here until 4:45 p.m."

Her dad had told them to be back by 6:00 p.m., and she wasn't trying to be too late. Laura was not quite as concerned with the time; her mama seemed to judge time by the streetlights. As long as she was in the house by the time they came on, she was good. The girls caught the 4:00 p.m. bus, and with all the stops, they got downtown about 4:25 p.m.

They decided to get something to eat at the Roses lunch counter and then walk home instead of waiting for the bus. The teen girls walked down Main Street toward Roses store full of smiles, ponytails swinging, and packages in hand.

Watching the time, the girls quickly ate and then made their way to the women's department. They wanted to get a couple of packages of the cotton bandannas. Both teens agreed that the bandannas the women wore on the tobacco farm would soak up the sweat better than their polyester headbands. While walking toward the hair accessories aisle, they saw a rotating rack full of bib overalls hung on clothes hangers.

"Want a pair of these?" Sydney joked.

"No, they look huge; I'll stick with my baggy jeans," Laura laughed.

It was after 5:30 p.m. when the girls finally started walking toward home. The day had gone by so fast. It was a good thing that they both had worn sneakers because they were walking and talking at a pretty swift pace. They took a shortcut through a couple of side streets instead of walking down to Mason Street where the bus would have let them off at the top of the hill. It saved them from having to walk down the hill by the school ballfield and playground.

When they reached the corner intersection, Laura said, "Girl, I spent a good chunk of my money, but today was so much fun!"

"Yes, it was great!" Sydney responded without breaking her pace. "I'll call you later!" she shouted back to Laura. Sydney would make it home a few minutes before 6:00 p.m.

As Laura opened the front door, Danielle jumped up from the couch and ran to meet her.

"What did you get for me?" She excitedly reached out to help Laura carry her bags.

"Oh, a little something pretty, you'll see," Laura said as she teasingly held the shopping bags up over her lil sis's head.

Her mama was sitting on the couch watching television. Looking up, she said, "Hey, Laura, did you have fun today?"

"Yes, ma'am, I bought a couple of things for school," Laura happily responded.

"OK, that's good. Can you go bring in that last set of clothes from the line for me before it gets too late?" her mama responded.

"Yes, ma'am," Laura answered and walked down the hallway to put up her bags. She was a little disappointed that her mama didn't seem too interested in her purchases. It was a little before 6:00 p.m., so there was a couple of hours of daylight time left. Laura knew that as long as she made it home before dusk dark, made good grades, and did her chores around the house, her mama rarely questioned her about anything. If Laura wasn't at her grandma's house, then she was at Sydney's house or down to the school playground with Danielle. Oh well, a little more interest or enthusiasm about her new purchases from her mama would be nice, Laura mused. Now, Grandma Annie was a different story. Tomorrow during Sunday dinner, Laura already knew that she was going to get plenty of questions about her purchases and day at the mall. Laura shook her head just thinking about it as she changed her shoes to go into the backyard.

Laura just barely remembered her dad. Mama had moved into this house a couple of streets over from Grandma Annie when Laura was in elementary school. She was about Danielle's age, now that she thought about it. Danielle was a toddler and always underfoot just like right now, Laura laughed because her lil sis was right there waiting for Laura to open the shopping bags.

"Come on, Danielle, help me bring in the clothes, then we'll open the shopping bags," Laura said, standing up from the bed.

Danielle followed Laura outside with the two clothes baskets. The lil girl folded the clothes as Laura took them down from the clothesline and handed them to her. Laura folded the big towels as she took them down. Laura still had a pile of freshly cleaned work clothes sitting in the center of her little twin bed. She moved them to the side to have room to show Danielle her purchases. Mama kept Danielle's hair in two to four ponytails, so the multicolored barrettes absolutely thrilled her lil sis. The little fashionista also liked Laura's hoops, holding them up to her ears in the mirror. Both girls fell onto the bed laughing.

Truly the fastest day of the week in their house was Sunday. John, Laura, and Danielle all rode the church bus to Sunday service. The service started at 11:00 a.m. so the bus usually picked them up around 10:30 a.m. A few people were already on the bus, and it still had to make a couple more stops before going to the church. Their mama made sure they went, even though most of the time she didn't go. Sometimes Grandma Annie would ride the bus to church. If Aunt Nicky was at church, usually arriving late, she would give them all a ride back home. If not, they rode the bus, and it usually got them back home around 1:30 p.m. or later. Deacon Harris was not nearly as punctual as Mr. Isaiah, Laura thought as she boarded the bus. Thank goodness the bus was air-conditioned because it was a sweltering hot July Sunday.

Deacon Harris dropped them back home at around 1:30 p.m. Laura knew that by 2:30 p.m. they would be on their way to Grandma Annie's for Sunday dinner. Laura could smell the aroma of the freshly fried chicken as she entered the house.

"Hey, how was church?" their mama hollered from the kitchen.

"It was good," John responded.

How would he know church was good, Laura thought, because he had been trading glances with Angie Brown throughout the service.

Laura didn't think he had heard a word the preacher said. John had convinced Mama to let him skip Sunday dinner at Grandma's so that he could catch the 3:30 p.m. matinee movie with friends. Friends was probably one friend name Angie Brown, Laura laughed to herself. John walked with them and carried the large platter of fried chicken over to Grandma's. As soon as they got there, he grabbed a napkin, two chicken legs, and was gone out the door. Everything smelled so good, and Laura was ready to eat. She filled her plate with potato salad, green beans, fresh corn on the cob, and Grandma Annie's oven-baked barbecue chicken. The food tasted just as delicious as it smelled. Laura decided that she would take a couple of pieces of the fried chicken for lunch tomorrow. Everybody was eating and enjoying the light conversation, which was mostly Grandma Annie talking about the morning service.

Then all of a sudden, Grandma Annie turned toward Laura and asked, "How was your Saturday at the mall; did you buy a lot of stuff?"

Laura was taking a drink of her sweet tea, so Danielle spoke up. "She got me some hair bows. See!" her lil sister said as she flipped her head back and forth. The three ponytails with barrettes on the end swung back and forth in the air. Everybody had a good laugh. "And she got some hoop earrings," Danielle continued.

"OK, that's enough," Mama interrupted her. "Let Laura speak for herself."

"I got a couple of pairs of jeans, a sundress, a jumper dress, and three tops that were on sale three for nine dollars," Laura proudly announced.

"Were those summer tops?" Grandma Annie asked.

"Yes, ma'am," Laura grimaced.

"Well, you know when you go back to school, the weather will be changing, and we won't have too many more hot days left for sundresses and little summer tops," her grandma stated. Turning to her daughter, Grandma Annie asked, "Gloria, did you take a look at what she purchased?"

Laura rarely heard anyone call her mama by her first name, Gloria.

Grandma Annie did not give her mama a chance to respond and continued with "You need to talk to Nicky. She can get Laura some nice things on discount at the Kress store."

No! No! No! Laura was screaming in her head.

Laura's mama let Grandma Annie finish, then she spoke up and said, "Mom, I'm working the 3:30 to midnight shift at the factory, and I'm not going to go walking around that mall with Laura. She knows that she needs a good winter coat, a few sweaters, pants, and some long-sleeve blouses for school. If she messes around there and squanders her money on nothing but summer clothes, then come winter she'll have to wear summer clothes."

"Don't worry," Laura chimed in trying to reassure everybody, "I'm making a shopping list to make sure I get everything I need for school."

"And put some of that tobacco money away for later," her grandma added.

"Yes, ma'am," Laura responded. Whew, that was close, she thought to herself.

"Hey, you all started without me?" Aunt Nicky came in and shouted from the living room. The layout of Grandma Annie's house was where the living room, dining room, and kitchen were one huge continuous room. A big dining table divided the living room from the kitchen. There was really no need for her aunt to shout, Laura thought to herself. Aunt Nicky dropped her purse on the couch and continued into the kitchen. She grabbed a plate and started dishing out some food for herself.

Ugh, I have got to get out of here before they start up on me and clothes again, Laura sighed to herself. "Mama, I'm finished; can I take Danielle down to Sydney's with me? I promised to take her to the playground for a little while," Laura asked.

"Yes, yes!" Danielle screamed with delight and was out of her seat taking her plate to the sink.

"Laura, how was your first week on the tobacco farm?" Aunt Nicky asked, taking a seat at the table. She continued, "I thought that I might see you in Kress yesterday. We were busy."

With a little trepidation in her voice, Laura gave her aunt a quick synopsis of her first week on the tobacco farm. It was also the first time her mama had heard Laura really talk about her experience on the farm. Then she went on to tell her about hanging out at the mall with Sydney on Saturday.

"That mall is expensive," Aunt Nicky responded with a little too much exaggeration in her voice for Laura.

"Oh, everything I got was on sale," Laura retorted. Except for the jumper dress, she thought to herself.

"Yeah, all on sale summer clothes," Grandma Annie started up again.

"Well, let me know what you want from Kress, and I'll get it for you on my employee discount," Aunty Nicky told her.

"OK, thanks, Aunt Nicky. Mama, can we go? It's already after 4:00pm."

"Yes," her mama responded. "Be back here in a couple of hours so that we can help your grandma clean up this kitchen."

As soon as Laura stepped out on to the front porch, she took a couple of breaths of fresh air. When Mama, Grandma, and Aunt Nicky got together on the same subject, *her,* it could be a lot. Even though everybody seemed to be perfectly OK with her brother, John, just dropping off the food and leaving to enjoy his Sunday. Boys' clothes were simple; all her brother ever wore was blue jeans, t-shirts, and button-down shirts, she reflected as she and Danielle joyfully walked toward Sydney's house.

"Hey, squirt," Sydney directed to Danielle. "I thought I was going to have to come looking for you all," she greeted them from the porch.

Laura laughed and said, "We were just finishing up dinner at my grandma's house, and you know our shopping yesterday was the main topic." Laura finished with a roll of her eyes.

"I bet," Sydney said. "I only had about $30 left, and my mom was glad she had me hold back that hundred dollars. I don't think Jacob spent any of his money."

The teen girls started walking to the playground with Danielle happily in the middle holding their hands. When they entered the school playground, Danielle let go of their hands and went running toward the swings and merry-go-round with her ponytails bouncing in the air.

"Be careful!" Laura shouted.

Sydney spotted Amy on the bleachers. She and Laura went and took a seat beside her. Laura kept a watchful eye on Danielle as the teens started to talk about their Saturday excursions. Turns out Amy had gone down to Main Street with Mike after his softball game. They went to Roses store and also the last matinee showing. Sydney and Laura teased Amy about spending time with Mike instead of hanging out with them at the mall. She insisted they were just friends because they only lived a few houses apart and had known each other forever. Laura and Sydney gave Amy a quirky sideways look. All three teen girls broke into laughter.

"Guess what?" Amy directed to the teens. "While we were in Roses, Mike bought a couple of pairs of those bib overalls and black long-sleeve t-shirts!"

"Girl! We saw them things in Roses too but decided to stick with our blue jeans," Laura responded.

"Well, I did buy a six-pack of those navy-blue tank-style t-shirts and a six-pack of men's large short-sleeve regular t-shirts. We got five more weeks on that tobacco farm, and I think those will work better," Amy told them.

"Well, just listen to you three sounding just like country farm girls," Carolyn said from behind them as she and Brenda laughed.

Oh, they get on my nerves, Laura thought. They always got something smart to say. She hadn't realized the annoying girls had come up and sat behind them.

"Your brother, Jacob, and Mike look especially good standing out in that ballfield with those nice dark country tans," Brenda directed to Sydney.

Laura knew the girls were just teasing with them, but Amy didn't seem to find it too funny.

"Why you three don't have nice tans like that?" Carolyn asked.

"Because we work under an overhang," Sydney responded.

The pickup game was ending, and it gave Laura a reason to get up and go check on Danielle. Sydney stood up to go with her.

"We'll see you all later," they both directed to Amy and the other girls. They knew Amy would go and greet Mike since the game was over.

"Come on, Danielle, it's time to go home," Laura shouted to her lil sis.

The three girls walked back home at a much slower pace, with Sydney and Laura talking about next week's work and what stories Mrs. Mary and the women probably had to tell them from the weekend. They actually enjoyed listening to the women talk.

The cleanup at Grandma Annie's was quick. Aunt Nicky was gone. Uncle Richard and his girls had already stopped by for a few minutes and were gone home also. John strolled in just in time to help carry some food back home. Looking at Grandma Annie pack up the chicken, Laura remembered that she had completely forgotten to buy a little mini-Igloo to take her lunch out to the tobacco farm.

"John," she asked her brother, "if I give you the money, can you get me a mini-insulated cooler or lunch container with a mini-ice pack tomorrow?"

"Laura, I have an extra insulated lunch bag that you can use," her mama interjected. "John, just get her two mini-ice packs so her lunch don't spoil out in that heat."

John agreed to get the ice packs at the grocery store tomorrow. Finally, Laura could take something other than PB&J sandwiches for lunch. But for tomorrow she would just take a couple of apples and some crackers.

The playground must have tuckered Danielle out because after her bath, she was sound asleep by the time Laura came into their bedroom from taking her shower. No storytelling tonight. Laura set her alarm clock for 6:00 a.m. and climbed into her own bed. She lay there looking up at the ceiling pondering the past week and the week ahead. She still had about $70 left, but Grandma Annie was right. She needed to be more strategic with her shopping because the new coat, pair of sneakers, and maybe a pair of boots was going to cost a lot. Laura dozed off to sleep feeling really good about her first weekend with real money.

WEEK 2 - GETTING IN THE GROOVE

Laura's startled eyes opened wide at the blaring sound of the 6:00 a.m. alarm clock. Frantically reaching for the off button, she was still not used to the alarm. Laura got up to start her second workweek on the tobacco farm. Those two days of sleeping in sure felt good, she thought as she finished her morning routine and started walking toward Sydney's house. Surveying the group as she approached the porch, Laura could tell that everyone had taken last week's work attire and the wet, dirty tobacco into consideration when getting dressed this morning. Jacob and Mike had on black long-sleeve t-shirts and bib overalls. Oh, they looked real country, Laura laughed to herself. Sydney and Laura had on blue jeans, dark-colored tank tops under a large, oversized long-sleeve button-down shirt. They had rolled the sleeves up to quarter length of their arms. But Amy had on a large, oversized dark blue man's t-shirt. The big short sleeves went down past her elbows and the bottom of the t-shirt reached her midthigh. All three of the teen girls wore cotton bandanas.

Mr. Isaiah pulled up right at 7:00 a.m. with his exuberant personality on full display even though the young crew was a little quiet and moving slow. As they got into the cargo bed of the truck, Laura noticed that Sydney and Jacob had a mini-Igloo instead of the two lunch boxes they carried last week. Amy and Mike had also switched from the children's cartoon lunch boxes to two insulated lunch bags. I guess we all want something for lunch other than PB&J sandwiches, she laughed to herself while taking a seat in the back of the truck. Riding out to the tobacco farm, Laura was actually looking forward to seeing Mrs. Mary and the crew. She wondered if Daniel and Anthony had won their softball games.

Pulling up at the tobacco barn to drop the girls off, Mr. Isaiah shouted out, "They all came back!" with a hint of teasing laughter in his loud, booming voice.

"Great, but I knew they would," Mrs. Mary greeted the young crew.

Mr. Isaiah shouted back as he turned the truck around and drove away. The girls waved to Jacob and Mike while greeting Mrs. Mary, Mrs. Cindy, and Miss Elaine. They settled into their positions around the worktable. Ugh, the teen girls wrinkled up their noses. The smell permeating from the tobacco leaves on the worktable was so strong. Mrs. Mary explained that Mr. Nate had pulled the truck into the barn over the weekend for safe keeping. The tobacco smell was super strong from the truck being closed up in that hot barn. Laura was glad they were working outside in the fresh air and really happy that Mrs. Mary and the women were already more than halfway finished with the load of tobacco.

"How was y'all weekend? Did you have fun at the mall?" Mrs. Cindy asked.

The girls were elated to tell the women about their weekend shopping excursion.

"I hope y'all didn't spend your whole week's pay," Mrs. Mary teased them good-naturedly.

"No, ma'am," they all responded in unison.

Everybody burst out into a good-hearted laugh. Laura knew she had spent well over half of her pay. She had calculated that with five more weeks to work, she would have a thousand dollars to spend on new school clothes! Of course, she still had to subtract out the money she was giving her mama toward the household expenses and to her brother, John, for lunch food.

The morning whizzed by as the girls got back into their stringing and looping rhythm. By the third truck swap out, their arms were really starting to feel the workout. They were looking forward to finishing the load of tobacco and taking a lunch break.

During the swap out, Sydney leaned over to Laura and whispered, "I bet you're looking forward to seeing Daniel."

Laura smiled and shrugged her shoulders. The girls laughed as they got back into position at the working table. The three women were, of course, working at a lightning speed pace. They were a little chatty but not as much as Laura thought they would be. Maybe Monday was a slow day for everybody.

Finally time for lunch, Laura gave out a sigh of relief as the two trucks came rolling down the road toward the barn. She had to admit to herself that she was a little anxious about seeing Daniel and hearing about his weekend. As everybody got their lunches from the back table, Laura asked Sydney about her mini-Igloo. It turned out that her brother, Jacob, had gotten it over the weekend. He had told their dad and mom that if he was going to work in the tobacco field for the next five weeks, then he needed more than a PB&J sandwich, apple, and chips for lunch. Knowing he was right, the girls laughed in agreement as they walked toward the shade trees. Laura saw Daniel walking slightly ahead of them carrying his family's cooler.

The young teen crew gathered under the shade tree in a semicircle. Daniel came and sat on the grass beside Laura with his plate of food.

"Hey, that's all you're eating?" he asked, seeing that she was only eating an apple.

"Yeah, I wasn't too hungry today, so I just brought a couple of apples and some crackers," she responded.

He offered her a piece of chicken, and Laura declined without even looking up. Laura didn't look up because she knew her face would reveal that she really did want that piece of chicken. Tomorrow she would have her icepacks and could bring some real food without worrying that it would spoil.

As Daniel was finishing up his plate of food, Laura turned toward him and mustered up the courage to ask about their softball game on Saturday. Daniel looked at her with that megawatt smile announcing that they had won their Saturday and Sunday games.

"Yeah, that Sunday game was awesome!" Anthony chimed in. "Did you see that catch Steve made in the outfield, cinching our win!"

And just like that, all the guys were focused on talking sports for the last few minutes of the lunch break.

The afternoon shift went by fast, and before Laura knew it, they were back in the cargo bed of Mr. Isaiah's truck soaking up the afternoon breeze. Mondays on the tobacco farm took a toll on everybody. Laura noticed that Amy's big man t-shirt seemed to have helped with keeping the dirt off her upper and lower body. She didn't look quite as dirty as Laura and Sydney did in their button-down shirts. Maybe she and Sydney should buy some big men's t-shirts, she pondered as Mr. Isaiah pulled up in front of Sydney's house at precisely 6:00 p.m. The girls woke up Jacob and Mike.

Slowly walking up the porch steps, Laura hollered into her grandma's screen door for Danielle.

"Hi, Laura," Grandma Annie greeted her at the door with Danielle in tow. "How was work today?"

"Hot, wet, and dirty," Laura responded. She was careful not to complain too much. "Grandma, what did you cook for dinner today?" Laura asked.

"Nothing, baby, you know Monday's dinner is Sunday's leftovers. Do you want me to fix you a plate?" her grandma asked.

"No, we got some leftovers at home. I was just thinking about lunch for this week," Laura explained. She knew that her mama usually cooked a couple of one-dish casseroles through the week, and Laura didn't want to take cold casserole for lunch.

"You didn't set aside any money to buy some lunch meat and fixings to make some sandwiches?" Grandma Annie asked. She continued, "Give John a few dollars and have him pick you up some lunch food from the grocery store."

"Yes, ma'am, I was planning to do that," Laura told her grandma.

"Anyways, tomorrow I'm cooking a little meatloaf, and I'll put a couple of slices aside for your lunch," her grandma said and winked at Laura.

Her Grandma Annie was tough and gentle all wrapped up in the same package. Laura smiled as she and Danielle started their trek home.

Laura had gotten Danielle settled into bed. She was trying her best to stay awake until John got in from work. It was almost 10:00 p.m. when she heard him coming in the front door. Taking the ten-dollar bill that she had placed under the alarm clock earlier, she got up and walked down the hallway.

"Hey, John, you got off a little late tonight," she greeted her brother.

"Yeah, we had to do some extra stocking from all the weekend grocery shoppers; the shelves were pretty bare. I got the mini-ice packs; I just put them in the freezer," John said.

"OK, thanks, can you pick me up a few things from the grocery store tomorrow? I made a little list, and here's a ten," Laura said while handing her brother the list and money.

"OK cool, I'll bring them tomorrow night," John said while glancing at the list. Laura had written loaf of bread, small pack of bologna, ham, turkey, small mustard, small mayo, and chips.

"How did today go on the tobacco farm?" he asked.

"It was OK; do you know if our recreational league softball teams ever play any teams outside the area?" Laura asked her brother.

"No, we just play other teams in our rec league. Why?" John asked.

"Nothing, just curious; thanks for getting my lunch stuff," Laura quickly responded and headed back to bed, not wanting to get too many questions from her brother about her sudden interest in rec league softball.

The next morning during the ride out to the tobacco farm, Sydney told Laura that her mom was going downtown today, so she asked her if she could go into Roses and get them a couple of packages of those big men's t-shirts. Both girls had agreed that the oversize men's t-shirts would be better than the button-down shirts. Laura mentally deducted that cost from her remaining cash. That first pay was dwindling.

The girls were back into their stringing and looping rhythm. Of course, not as fast as Mrs. Mary and the women but definitely steadier than on Monday. Mrs. Mary and Mrs. Cindy were teasing Miss Elaine because she and Mr. Kevin had come together to the weekend cookout. Miss Elaine had apparently brought her special potato salad, and Mr. Kevin was giving her all kinds of accolades in front of everybody. From what Laura could garner from their conversation, Miss Elaine was a widow whose husband had passed quite a while ago. She had two elementary-age children and lived in her own house on a plot of land next to her parents and some other siblings. It reminded Laura of how close they lived to Grandma Annie, even though they didn't own a plot of land and rented their houses.

Everybody was ready for a break and sped up a little bit to finish the truck before the guys rolled in for lunch. Today, Laura had two chicken legs, an apple, chips, and a juice box for lunch. She was ready to eat and was hoping to sit beside Daniel again. But not today—she ended up sitting in between Amy and Sydney. She always sat beside

Sydney, but Amy took the other spot on her right side on the grass. Mike sat down on the opposite side of Amy. Daniel ended up sitting slightly across from her beside his brother, David Jr. She still had a good view of him. His brother, David Jr., didn't talk much except about sports; they were already talking about the upcoming high school and professional football season. Laura wondered why David Jr. was working in tobacco and not a regular summer job because he was a senior, just like her brother, John. At that moment Laura looked up from her thoughts and caught Daniel's eyes gazing at her. She smiled, and he smiled back with that mesmerizingly dimpled grin. His baseball cap was turned backward so she had a full view of his face. He was handsome.

"Girl, where your mind at because you didn't hear a word I just said?" Sydney said to Laura.

"I was just enjoying this chicken," Laura tried to play it off. "It sure is better than a PB&J sandwich."

That forty-five minutes went by so fast, it felt like a five-minute lunch break. As they were walking back to the barn, Daniel walked up beside Laura and Sydney.

"I see you were a little hungrier today," he said jokingly to Laura.

She couldn't help but laugh. Sydney walked up just a little ahead of them.

"Today is going to be a long day," Daniel commented.

"All of them are long," Laura responded.

"Yeah, but today Anthony and I have softball practice; we practice on Tuesdays and Thursdays, so it's going to be extra-long," Daniel explained.

"And hot," Laura added as they reached the barn working area.

They both laughed. Their little conversations seemed to flow easily.

The teen girls and older women processed the afternoon trucks at a steady rhythmic pace. During the ride home, Sydney leaned over and whispered to Laura, "I saw Daniel trying to get in some talk time with you. I think he really likes you, and he is easy on the eyes."

Both girls started to giggle.

"What are you all laughing at?" Amy asked.

"How we all look like country folks coming in from the fields all dirty and tired on the back of this truck," Laura answered.

All three girls burst into laughter as Mr. Isaiah pulled up in front of Sydney's house.

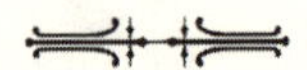

Later that evening, after showering and changing into her pajamas, Laura settled on the couch to watch some television with Danielle. Suddenly, there was a knock at the door. Both girls looked up because no one came to their house in the evenings. Laura walked to the door and peeped out the curtain; it was Sydney. Laura opened the door, and Sydney greeted her with a big "Hey, girl!"

"Hi, Sydney," Danielle greeted her, peeping from behind Laura.

"Hey, squirt," Sydney greeted the little girl while coming into the living room and taking a seat on the couch. "You left before my mom could give you the pack of t-shirts, so I told her that I'd bring them over so that we can wear them tomorrow," Sydney explained while handing the Roses bag to Laura.

Pulling out the package of navy-blue men's t-shirts, Laura saw that they were extra-large. Sydney saw her looking at the tag and explained how she had already tried one on and the t-shirt sleeves came down about a quarter length her arm. They wouldn't have to keep rolling up the sleeves like they do on the button-down shirts. Laura took one of the t-shirts out of the packaging. She stood up and held it against her body. It came down to her thighs, which should help keep her pants drier.

"How much do I owe your mom?" Laura asked Sydney.

"Nothing, my mom said she got them for us, no charge," Sydney responded with a smile.

Mrs. Wilson was really nice and thoughtful. Laura made a mental note to thank her tomorrow because that saved her a few dollars.

Sydney and Laura chatted for a few more minutes, then Sydney went home. Both girls knew they had an early morning.

Wednesday and Thursday went like clockwork. They had all gotten into the routine of getting up early, working on the tobacco farm all day, going to bed early, and then repeating the process the next day. All three teen girls had morphed into their own little uniform of bandanas, jeans, tank tops, and oversized men's t-shirts as a large cover-up from the wet and dirty tobacco.

Laura had not seen her mama all week again. She didn't know how the guys still managed to play softball. It was enough for her just to get Danielle fed, bathed, and in bed. She had not had the energy to take her lil sis up to the playground since Sunday. Laura decided to do something with the lil girl on Saturday since she and Sydney were not going to the mall. They had decided not to spend their whole pay at the mall but wait and check out Sunday's sales flyers in the newspaper.

Friday and their second payday! The atmosphere was always different on Fridays. Even though the women were happy and talked while working throughout the whole week, Laura noticed that they were particularly jovial on Fridays. Everybody was looking forward to the weekend.

"You girls going back out to that mall to do some more shopping this weekend?" Mrs. Mary asked.

"Ah, we might just go downtown to Main Street or to the mall food court to hang out with some friends. I'm going to save most of my money until August and catch some of those back-to-school sales," Laura responded.

"Me too," Amy and Sydney responded almost simultaneously.

"That's good," Mrs. Cindy chimed in. "It ain't much, but I know y'all parents got you putting a little something back for savings and school activities. Our boys are involved in so many sports and activities that we'd go broke if we didn't have them put a little to the side."

"I know we're having Anthony save some of his pay," Mrs. Mary added.

Mrs. Cindy continued, "Yeah, David Jr. got his driver's license, and he's saving up for a little car or truck. We'll probably drop them off or let them use the truck to go to the mall in town. Those boys like their sneakers and are already talking about getting some new ones."

Laura and Sydney looked at each other when Mrs. Cindy made the "drop them off at the mall" comment.

"Whew, it's almost lunchtime. Girls, I brought y'all an end-of-week treat," Mrs. Mary announced with a smile. "A freshly baked pound cake straight out of the oven this morning."

Miss Elaine exclaimed, "Girls, y'all are in for a treat cause Mary makes the best melt-in-your-mouth pound cake…no frosting needed."

Everybody laughed as they finished the last few tobacco leaves from the third truck. Laura was hungry; those two pieces of toast she had for breakfast were long digested. Her mouth was salivating at the thought of a nice slice of freshly baked pound cake.

Oh, it felt good to the teens to take a break and sit under the shade tree. Laura had noticed David Jr. and Daniel walking a little faster to get their family cooler situated under the adult tree, get their lunch out, and then come over to the teen tree. Laura thought, maybe he was trying to hurry up so that he could get a seat beside her on the grass. They didn't always end up sitting beside each other, but they always got in a few minutes of conversation before starting the afternoon shift. Today, he sat beside her.

"My mom baked a pound cake for us," Anthony proudly announced as Mrs. Mary handed out slices of cake. There were two slices in each plastic sandwich bag. Just like Mrs. Mary to be so thoughtful of the fact that they would be eating outside. Instead of eating her bologna sandwich, Laura took the fried bologna out of the bread and ate it with her pound cake.

"Oh, I'll have to try that combo sometime, fried bologna and pound cake," Daniel teased her with his easy grin.

Grandma Annie baked some good cakes, but the women were right about Mrs. Mary's pound cake melting in your mouth. Laura wanted another piece but didn't want to look greedy in front of Daniel. She decided that she'd ask Mrs. Mary for another piece during their 3:00 p.m. truck swap out.

"Come on y'all, let's get moving, here comes Isaiah and Nate!" hollered Mr. Roy Smith. Everybody was moving swiftly, ready for the second half of the day to be over and the start of the weekend. Mrs. Mary had also set aside a basket of sliced cake for Mr. Isaiah and the rest of the crew.

"See y'all in a few hours," Daniel said as he walked off with the guys to get into the truck.

Laura could have sworn that even though they were all standing there, Daniel was looking directly at her. Her face felt flushed—must be the blazing heat.

The afternoon shift and tobacco truck rotations went swiftly. Laura and the girls asked Mrs. Mary for a piece of her pound cake when they took their quick 3:00 p.m. break. They ate it with a few sips of water while Mr. Nate rotated out the tobacco trucks. This would be their last truck of the day. Everybody was working in rhythm to finish on time; it was almost the weekend!

With his precision timing, Mr. Isaiah and the crew came driving down the dirt road around 5:15 p.m. Jacob and Mike went to get the lunch containers. Mr. Isaiah walked up and handed the empty basket to Mrs. Mary and thanked her on behalf of the crew for the delicious pound cake. He then handed out the white envelopes to the girls. Laura folded hers in half, placed it in her jeans pocket, and then patted her pocket for assurance.

"Thanks again for the cake, Mrs. Mary!" all five of them said and waved as they jumped into the cargo bed of the truck.

They had finished their second week on the tobacco farm. Laura was in her thoughts as they sat back and enjoyed the breeze blowing into the back of the truck. Daniel was in the eleventh grade; she wondered if he had a girlfriend that came out to watch him play softball on the weekends. She wouldn't mind going to one of his and Anthony's rec league games, but that required transportation and her transportation was the city bus. Her brother, John, was a senior; she pondered if he was saving up for a car like David Jr. He had talked about going into the military after high school. By the time they pulled up in front of Sydney's house, the slightest drizzle of rain had started to fall.

"OK, you young folks, hurry and get home before this rain starts up. I'll see you bright and early Monday morning!" Mr. Isaiah shouted from the cab of the truck as he waved to Mrs. Wilson.

They all said quick goodbyes and headed home. Nobody was trying to get caught in the rain to get their dirty tobacco clothes even more wet and sticky on their bodies. The rainfall had picked up in the few minutes that it had taken Laura to walk the few houses down to her grandma. She sat down in one of the porch rocking chairs. The rain had slightly cooled the air, and it felt good. Laura just leaned back and sunk into the rocking chair.

"Laura, Laura, how long have you been sitting out here?" she heard her Grandma Annie saying as she was coming out of a groggy fog.

"Child, you must have sat out here and went to sleep; I was looking out the door to see if you was coming down the street because it's a little past 6:30 p.m.," her grandma said.

"What!" Laura said, sitting up. She had slept over thirty minutes. The rain was still coming down but had slacked up a little.

"They must really be working my little tobacco girl out on that farm; well, at least today is Friday." Grandma Annie continued, "Danielle's sitting at the kitchen table eating a hotdog and fries. Do you want some dinner?"

"No, ma'am, but I'm going to sit right here and let her finish eating," Laura said while leaning back in the rocker.

Grandma Annie sat down in the other rocker. "Are you all right?" she asked Laura.

"Yes, Grandma, I'm just a little tired from standing all day. Working outside in that tobacco ain't no joke," Laura responded.

"I know, child," Grandma Annie said. "Years ago, before your mama, Aunt Nicky, and Uncle Richard was even born, we worked picking cotton for extra money."

"What, Grandma! When?" Laura sat straight up in the rocking chair.

"In South Carolina before the family moved up here to North Carolina. It was back-breaking work. We all got regular jobs when we moved here to Ervinsville. This is where I met your Grandpa Larry. Your mama ain't never been out to the country. I was kinda surprised when she agreed to let you work on the tobacco farm."

"Oh wow, Grandma, I didn't know. You never talked about living in South Carolina. We're standing with our arms and hands moving all day. But it's OK because the people are really nice and, Grandma, I want my own money," Laura said, subconsciously touching her pants pocket. She continued, "It's only for this summer because next year, I'll have a regular worker's permit."

"OK, you know your mama's doing her best," Grandma Annie emphasized. "Divorce is hard on families. Don't spend all your money this summer; hold some back for school activities. You know you're starting high school."

"Yes, ma'am," Laura said.

All the adults and her brother, John, kept giving her the same advice; don't spend all your money. Laura groaned as she got up from the rocking chair. Danielle came out onto the porch, and the sisters headed home while the rain had let up a little.

WASHOUT WEEKEND

The rain continued throughout the night, and Laura awoke to the sound of rain still tapping on the roof and windows. She didn't even remember John or Mama coming into the house last night. Her mama and grandma always said sleep was better when it was raining outside. But now it was Saturday morning, and Laura was wide awake, staring up at the ceiling hoping the rain would stop.

"Hey, Laura, you up?" Danielle asked as she got out of her bed and into her sister's bed. Laura glanced at the clock, and it was only a little after 7:00 a.m. She rolled over, put her arms around her little sister, and they both dozed back off to sleep for a couple more hours.

Laura hated rainy Saturdays because it meant either doing no laundry or doing a little laundry and hanging it up in the bathroom to dry. Well, I've got to at least get my work clothes washed, she sighed as she and Danielle got up for the day. Laura hung her work clothes on hangers on the shower curtain rod. Those wet jeans were heavy; she hoped they wouldn't break the rod and fall all over the bathroom floor. Laura thoroughly cleaned the bathroom and their bedroom while Danielle entertained herself with Saturday morning cartoons.

It was almost noon when her mama finally emerged from her bedroom. She was still in her housecoat.

"Oh, that rain put me out," she greeted them. "Looks like it has settled in for the day."

"Morning, Mama. I hope it slacks up enough so that I can walk to Roses," Laura said.

Laura wanted to get a pack of the thinner boy's black tank shirts. Amy had told them that they were lighter weight than the regular tank tops and fit better under the big t-shirts. On Friday evening, when she counted out her money, Laura took out the $40 and put it in a small envelope. She had placed it on her mama's night table. Her mama was busily getting the coffee pot brewing when the phone rang. Laura went to answer it.

"Hello. Hey, Sydney. OK, bye. Here, Laura, it's Sydney," Danielle announced, handing the phone to her sister.

Laura took the whole phone and walked back to the bedroom with the extra-long cord. "Hey, girl, can you believe it's still raining?" she greeted Sydney.

"I know, those clouds are heavy and settled in; I think it might rain all day," Sydney greeted her and continued with "My mom already said that I can't go to the mall today, she said it's too nasty outside."

"What a bummer," Laura interjected. "I wanted to go to Roses. They don't close until 7:00 p.m. If the rain stops by three or four o'clock, maybe we can still go," Laura said with a little hope in her voice.

"Oh, my mom's calling me; I think she's going to have me cleaning the whole house today," Sydney said and laughed. "I'll call you back later."

It turned out to be a really long, slow Saturday with Laura cleaning the house and watching cartoons with Danielle. The two girls did have a good time laughing and dancing to *Soul Train* and *American Bandstand.* But the day was still dragging on with the steady rain. John had gotten up and left for work. Saturday was busy at the grocery store whether it rained or not. Mama had stayed in her housecoat and in her bedroom pretty much all day. Laura was actually looking forward to church tomorrow just to get out of the house. She knew the church bus was coming rain or shine.

The heavy downpour had finally turned into a light, but still steady, rain by the time they woke up on Sunday morning. Grandma Annie didn't come to church. If the weather was bad, she usually stayed home because she didn't want to catch no colds or other sickness. Laura rarely remembered her grandma ever being sick.

By the time they got back home from church and changed clothes, the rain had slowed down to a drizzle. They walked over to their grandma's house using umbrellas. With those extra hours at home, Grandma Annie had cooked up a storm because all kinds of delicious smells greeted them at the front door. Aunt Nicky also came over for dinner but not Uncle Richard and the girls. Laura thought that the rain must have kept them home.

What a washout weekend, Laura mused as they walked home from Grandma Annie's on Sunday evening. The rain had finally come to a full stop as the sun was setting, but it had left a steamy, muggy July heat. Laura wondered if they had a washout weekend in Herd, since it was only about thirty miles outside the city. If they had rain that tobacco was going to be even more wet, she thought with a groan. It didn't matter, Laura was still looking forward to going back to work on the tobacco farm tomorrow.

"Laura," her mom interrupted her thoughts as they were walking home, "I'm going to do some laundry tomorrow before going to work, so when you get in tomorrow afternoon, bring the clothes in from the line."

You have got to be kidding me, Laura screamed inside as she responded, "Yes, ma'am."

She knew that in addition to working at the grocery store, her brother kept their yard and Grandma Annie's yard cut. She really didn't mind bringing in the laundry, just not after a long, hot day on the tobacco farm.

As soon as they walked into the house, John announced that since it finally stopped raining, he was going to go up the street and hang out with some friends for a couple of hours.

"Yeah, a friend named Angie Brown and her front porch," Laura said under her breath.

"OK, John, just don't be out too late," Mama responded.

He was gone out the door before anything else could be said. After helping her mama put away the food, Laura picked up the phone and went to her bedroom to call Sydney. Danielle was snuggled up under Mama on the couch watching television.

THE HALFWAY POINT

Monday morning and not a drop of rain in the sky. Laura looked up at the clear blue sky with the sun already in full appearance for the day. From their conversation last night, according to Sydney, Mr. Isaiah and his wife were at church yesterday. Sydney hadn't seen her parents talking to them, so she wasn't sure if Herd had a rain washout weekend or not.

Everybody was already on the porch as Laura approached Sydney's house and in great moods for a Monday. They were all just happy to be outside from being couped up in the house all weekend. It had been a very long, slow, wet weekend. Jacob and Mike's rec league softball games were canceled so they would have a couple of makeup games added to the end of the summer schedule. The teens saw the big, black, shining truck turn the corner and knew it was time to start tobacco workweek three.

Listening to Mr. Isaiah greet Mr. Wilson, the teens overheard Mr. Isaiah talking about the amount of rain that fell in Herd. It had rained just about all weekend. The teens knew that meant the tobacco was going to be soaking wet this morning. Jacob and Mike looked at each other and groaned as they climbed into the back of the truck. Laura and the girls giggled, knowing the two guys would be very wet and dirty by lunchtime. Those bib overalls weren't going to help too much today.

The girls did a quick wave to Jacob and Mike as Mr. Isaiah turned the truck around and headed back up the dirt road out to the tobacco fields. That first truckload of tobacco was nauseatingly smelly from all the rain and being shut up in the hot, humid barn all weekend! Laura was glad she only had toast for breakfast and that the women were over halfway finished with the first truck.

"Wow, this is messy!" Laura commented as they started stringing and looping the second truckload of tobacco.

"Yeah, the leaves are really wet so that makes the bundle feel a little heavier, and when you make the loop, it definitely wets up your whole upper body," Mrs. Mary laughed.

The three women continued with their looping rhythm like it was nothing. They chatted about how their gardens really needed the rain. Then Mrs. Mary commented about how she couldn't hang out the laundry this weekend, so their clothes dryer got a good workout. Laura's ears perked up. Mrs. Cindy also added to the conversation. She started talking about how each time David Sr. and her two boys, David Jr. and Daniel, changed work clothes it was almost a full load of laundry.

With heightened interest, Laura spoke up and asked, "So, you use your washer and dryer a couple of times a week?"

"Oh no," Mrs. Cindy responded. "I usually do a load of work clothes on Wednesday evening and again on Saturday morning. We hang them out to dry. I don't use that dryer unless it's raining or icy cold outside. We're not trying to get no super high electric bill."

"I know that's right," Miss Elaine chimed in. "Your clothes smell so nice and fresh when you hang them outside in the sunshine."

Laura was looping and thinking about what the women had said about using the clothes dryer. Saturday was laundry day at her house. She knew that Sydney's family had a dryer and so did Grandma Annie, even though both families hardly ever used them. Everybody in Laura's neighborhood had at least two clotheslines running in their backyards. But a clothes dryer sure would be nice, she thought as her hands grabbed another bunch of wet tobacco leaves. The teen girls were dirtier than usual and very wet.

Laura was glad they were starting the third truck, which meant it would soon be time for lunch. She was ready for a real break. It was taking longer to finish the wet loads of tobacco, so they barely got a minute break during the truck swap outs. They finished the third tobacco truck just as the two midday trucks were turning down the dirt road, signaling the lunch break. Laura, Sydney, and Amy quickly ran out to the outhouse to wash their face and hands. Walking back to the barn, Laura noticed that the guys were carrying some extra folding chairs. They took them to the teen lunch tree.

"There was a lot of rain this weekend, so my dad thought it would be a good idea to bring some extra folding chairs," David Jr. explained to the group of teens.

"Yeah, they're from our church fellowship hall," Daniel chimed in as they placed the eight chairs in a semicircle.

Daniel made sure he sat beside Laura. The guys were eating and complaining about how wet the tobacco field was today and also missing their softball games over the weekend.

"Your mom said that y'all went to the gym and played some basketball since your games were a washout," Laura slightly turned and said to Daniel. She found it easier to turn and talk to him from the chair. Sitting and turning on the grass to talk directly to him always seemed a little awkward.

"Yeah, it was fun, just a few pickup games but it got us out of the house for a few hours," Daniel responded. "What did you do this weekend?" he asked.

"Not too much, a lot of housework and entertained my little sister," Laura responded.

"Yep, all that rain was a real bummer," Daniel said.

Wow, those were my exact words to Sydney when we talked on the phone last night, Laura remembered. "Yes, it was," she answered Daniel with a smile.

"Yep, it sure was," Anthony interjected from the other side of Daniel.

The guys started talking about having to play double softball games on one of the upcoming weekends before the season was over. Laura didn't care that the guys' conversation had shifted back to sports. She liked listening to Daniel talk. He had a smooth, deep-sounding, distinct voice. I guess to match that dimpled megawatt smile, she thought to herself.

"OK, young folks, let's get ready for the afternoon shift," Mrs. Mary roused them.

Laura stood up and started to fold up her chair. But Daniel reached out and took her and Sydney's chairs. Walking with Laura and Sydney, he carried their chairs back to the barn. Laura saw Mike ahead of them carrying two chairs with Amy walking beside him. She touched Sydney's arm and nodded her head in their direction. Both girls gave each other a knowing glance.

There was going to be no dry loads of tobacco today! The fourth truckload was just as wet as the first truckload. Only one more load to go and Monday's workday would be over.

Taking a quick break while Mr. Nate got the fifth truck into position, Laura and the girls talked about how nice it was of Mrs. Cindy's husband, Mr. David Sr., to think about them and bring those extra folding chairs. They hoped he would leave them in the barn because it sure felt better than sitting on the ground.

"Yep, because I don't think I could have gotten up off that ground today," Sydney said.

"I know, it's the same amount of tobacco, but my arms sure feel like it's a whole lot more."

All three girls laughed in agreement. By the end of Monday, they all looked a frightful mess.

"My, my, my!" Mrs. Wilson greeted them. "Isaiah, these young folks look like they had a rough day."

"Yeah, them fields were really wet today with all the weekend rain, but tomorrow will be better. See y'all in the morning!" Mr. Isaiah shouted, never turning off his truck and was gone back to the country.

"I'm really proud of you all for sticking with it. You know this is week three, so you're practically halfway through the harvesting season. It's laborious work harvesting and stringing tobacco, I've done it myself many, many years ago, and I'm sure the process is pretty much the same," Mrs. Wilson said to the teens.

"Yes, ma'am," The teens responded with a laugh. They were really happy to get positive accolades from Mrs. Wilson.

"OK, I'll see y'all tomorrow," Laura said as she started toward Grandma Annie's house. Walking away, she laughed at herself realizing that she was starting to say y'all instead of you all, just like Mrs. Mary and them.

Laura stopped and took a minute to carefully pull the big t-shirt over her head. She didn't want that dirt getting all over her face. The extra-large t-shirts did provide pretty good coverage. It was almost like wearing one of her grandma's big muumuu dresses on top of her regular clothes. Laura laughed out loud. Grandma only had four steps leading up to her porch, but today it felt like twenty steps.

Laura was trying her best to fast walk Danielle home. Oh gosh, here they come again. It was Carolyn and Brenda. Eric wasn't with them this time. Laura was tired and knew she still had clothes to bring in from the line.

"Hey, Laura, we're on our way up to the schoolyard for a quick pickup softball game since it rained all weekend. Why don't you and your little sister come up?" Carolyn greeted her.

"Girl, she probably tired from working in that tobacco field all day," Brenda added.

"No, not today, maybe we'll walk up there another day this week," Laura answered without breaking her stride.

"Yeah, right," she heard them say and laugh as they continued on their way.

From her grandma's house to the corner was only four houses, at the corner she turned right, walked up two blocks on Elwood Road where there were no houses and then turned right down her street, Pinewood. Why was she always encountering these super annoying girls on this little strip of road? she seethed.

"Are we going to walk up to the playground?" Danielle asked as they turned down their street. Her lil inquisitive sis was definitely listening to the conversation between Laura and the neighborhood girls.

"Maybe tomorrow, because today we've got to bring in this laundry," Laura reminded Danielle.

"OK, I helped Mama hang the clothes out this morning," Danielle announced with delight in her voice.

"And now you can help me bring them in," Laura said and laughed while tickling her lil sis.

Laura slept like a rock straight through the night until the alarm clock woke her up. She had folded and put away all the clothes last night. If we had a clothes dryer, I could have done all that laundry while we were stuck in the house this past weekend, she muttered to herself as she went into the bathroom.

The tobacco was definitely not quite as wet on Tuesday, and by Wednesday it was back to its normal dampness level. Laura was glad that Mr. David Sr. had indeed left the extra folding chairs in the barn. Each day Daniel grabbed three folding chairs. They would sit beside each other with Sydney to her right and Anthony to Daniel's left. The lunch conversations flowed back and forth quite smoothly even though the lunch break still seem to zoom by in mere minutes.

They were finishing up the fifth and final truck of the day. The guys had not come in from the tobacco field for the day yet.

"Maybe we are actually getting faster," Laura announced as they finished bundling the last few tobacco leaves.

"Oh, you get faster without even realizing it," Mrs. Mary said. "It's all in the steady rhythm, and your hands getting used to the feel of about ten to fifteen big tobacco leaves."

The girls sat up on the worktable and untied their bandannas. The cotton scarves definitely held the sweat back better than the polyester headbands they had worn the first week.

"Elaine, what you fixing for your man's dinner tonight?" Mrs. Cindy teased her.

Miss Elaine just shook her head incredulously at Mrs. Cindy and said, "Y'all are too much!"

The girls and women all laughed. Laura could tell the women had been friends for a long time, just like her and Sydney. About that time, they heard the familiar sound of the three trucks turning down the dirt road. Two more days to Friday, Laura sighed as she jumped off the worktable.

Oh boy, Laura thought as she approached her grandma's house at the end of the workday. She could see Danielle waiting for her on the porch. Laura had managed to put her off yesterday from going to the playground, but she knew that was not going to work this Wednesday afternoon.

"Hey, Laura, are we going to walk up to the playground?" Danielle greeted her.

Even though she was bone tired, Laura figured that a quick midweek walk to the playground would be good. "Yes, we can go, but I have to shower and change clothes first."

"Yeah!" the little girl screamed and almost fell jumping up out of the porch rocking chair.

Grandma Annie came out to see what all the commotion was about. Laura told her about their little excursion up to the school playground for about an hour.

"OK, but be back home before it gets dark and call and let me know that you're home," she instructed Laura.

Laura rung Sydney as soon as she got in the house. Sydney was incredulous that Laura actually wanted to walk up to the playground after the three days of processing wet tobacco they just had. But she still agreed to go after Laura assured her they were not staying long. Just long enough to let Danielle run off some energy because she had been couped up in the house. Danielle was elated and could barely wait for Laura to shower and change clothes.

"OK, we're only staying about thirty minutes," Laura shouted a reminder to Danielle as she ran toward the merry-go-round. There were a few people playing softball, but Laura and Sydney were not interested in watching the game today. They walked toward the empty side of the bleachers and sat down. It was already about seven o'clock, and there was the slightest breeze in the air.

Sydney leaned back on the bleachers and said, "Ah, I didn't think I was going to make it. I'm sure glad that Daniel's dad left those folding chairs for us. I see you and Daniel having your own little conversations at lunchtime."

"Me either, my legs felt that walk up here," Laura answered and continued nonchalantly, "Girl, he's all right." Laura visualized Daniel's face and smiled.

"But you know we're all going to different high schools," Sydney commented.

"I know, and he's so handsome with those dimples, he probably has a girlfriend," Laura responded. She had already wondered about that herself.

"Hey, what are you two doing sitting way down here?" Eric said as he walked up to them.

Eric was a year ahead of them in the eleventh grade, just like Anthony and Daniel. He was friends with Jacob, and they all played on the softball team together with Laura's brother, John.

"Just relaxing while Danielle playing on the swings. We're getting ready to head back home in a minute," Laura said as she stood up. Sydney stood up too. "Oh, Sydney, you can wait here, I'm just going to get Danielle; I'll be right back," Laura said as she ran toward the swings.

Laura pushed Danielle on the swings for a few minutes, allowing time for Eric and Sydney to talk.

"Girl, why did you leave me alone with Eric?" Sydney asked as they walked home.

"I think he likes you because he always makes a point to talk to us when he sees us at the playground. Even though I have seen him walking with Carolyn and Brenda a few times," Laura explained.

"Those two," Sydney said and rolled her eyes at the thought of them.

The girls continued talking about boys and clothes with Danielle happily in the middle, holding each of their hands until they reached the corner intersection at Pinewood and Elwood. It was a little past 8:00 p.m. and getting dark. The streetlights were coming on as Laura and Danielle walked into their house.

The third week was a blur, but especially Thursday. Laura didn't know about Sydney, but she sleepwalked through the whole workday. That midweek excursion to the school playground was not going to happen again until after they finished working on the tobacco farm for the summer. Her twelve-hour days started with the 6:00 a.m. alarm clock and ended when Mr. Isaiah dropped them back home at 6:00 p.m. And Laura's day didn't even end there, nope, tiredness was really kicking her butt today. Danielle will have to read me a bedtime story tonight, she laughed to herself as they rode in the back of the truck toward home.

"Wake up!" Amy shouted. "We're here."

Jacob and Mike were dozing as usual, but Laura and Sydney had also dozed off to sleep leaning against each other. It had been a long day, and the breeze felt good. Everybody laughed as they jumped out of the back of the truck.

Fridays were becoming the something special day, and the teen crew was not disappointed when Miss Elaine brought out a large tray of chocolate brownies. She had precut and sorted the brownies into plastic lunch bags. She also had a second tray of pecan brownies. Miss Elaine explained that she didn't know if any of the teens had nut allergies, so she separated the brownies. Laura took one of each kind and enjoyed eating every morsel. They tasted like heaven was melting in her mouth with every bite. She was catching side glances of Daniel, and he was really enjoying the brownies too. He had also gotten one of each kind, and in three bites they were gone.

"Boy, Miss Elaine and Mrs. Mary can really bake. I don't know which one I like the most, the pound cake or the brownies," Laura said, turning to Daniel.

He laughed and said, "Yeah, they were both pretty good. My mom is a really good cook, and I'm sure she'll bring something out here before the summer's over." Laura could hear the admiration in his voice.

"I'm sure she is," Laura responded with a smile. She wondered what Mrs. Cindy's specialty was as she looked forward to another Friday treat. PB&J or lunch meat, an apple, and chips were her normal lunch.

Mr. Kevin James, who was usually pretty quiet, spoke up as they were starting to clean up the lunch area. He said to the group, "Those were some mighty fine brownies weren't they, just melt right in your mouth."

Mrs. Mary and Mrs. Cindy looked at each other and cracked up with laughter. Laura knew that Miss Elaine was going to get plenty of good-natured ribbing this afternoon. But Mr. Kevin was right about them brownies being melt-in-your-mouth good.

The afternoon shift and tobacco truck rotations went quickly. Miss Elaine definitely took some teasing from Mrs. Mary and Mrs. Cindy. It seemed like she and Mr. Kevin had a movie date planned for Saturday night. Laura had never been on a date before. Actually, she thought, I have never had a boyfriend.

Finally, like clockwork, the three trucks came down the dirt road, signaling the end of week three on the tobacco farm. Mr. Isaiah handed out the white envelopes to the girls. Laura folded hers in half, placed it in her jeans pocket and then patted her pocket for reassurance. She breathed another sigh of relief as they jumped into the back of the truck. Laura and her friends had made it halfway through the tobacco harvest season.

MAIN STREET WEEKEND

Laura stood at the chest of drawer holding her money envelope. After giving her mom this week's $40, she had a total of $380. She hadn't spent any money since the first payday weekend. Laura took $80 and some loose change and put it into her little crossbody purse. She put the envelope with the remaining $300 back under her clothes in the top drawer and closed it. Laura wasn't planning on doing a lot of shopping this weekend. Since last weekend was a washout and she didn't get take Danielle down to Main Street, they were going to go today. But first, she had to wash and hang out her work clothes.

"Mama, have you ever considered getting a clothes dryer?" Laura asked as she came in from hanging her work clothes on the line.

"No," her mama responded while drinking her coffee at the kitchen table. "I don't have clothes dryer money, and it will run up the electric bill."

"If we only used it on rain weekends and extremely cold days, it shouldn't cost too much," Laura responded.

"Laura, you already know that sometimes during the winter when it's really cold we go over to your grandma's house and use her washer and dryer to do the large laundry," her mama countered.

"Yes, ma'am," she responded to her mama. But thought to herself, yeah and we hang all the regular clothes in the bathroom when the weather is bad. Not to mention all the times I've brought in frozen clothes from the line, Laura muttered as she went to get dressed for today's Main Street outing.

Twining in blue jean shorts, tank tops, and sneakers, Laura and Danielle entered the kitchen.

"We're ready to go!" Danielle announced with a huge grin.

Sipping on her second cup of coffee and eating a couple of slices of toast, their mama looked up and smiled at her daughters.

"Be careful," she directed to Laura as the girls excitedly started their Saturday outing.

Standing at the corner intersection, Sydney was waiting for them to come outside. The two girls had decided the night before to meet at 10:30 a.m. to walk up the hill and catch the 11:00 a.m. bus downtown. Danielle saw Sydney when they stepped out onto the porch and took off running toward her with those ponytails and barrettes flying in the air.

"Hey, squirt." Sydney hugged the little girl as Laura came walking up to them.

Danielle was so excited to be hanging out with her big sister and Sydney that she happily entertained them with talk all the way to the bus stop and the whole bus ride downtown.

Even though the mall had been open for almost five years, a lot of people still shopped on Main Street. Getting off the bus, Sydney asked, "Do you want to go in Kress?"

Before Laura could say no, Danielle squealed, "Yes! Yes! My Aunt Nicky works in there."

The three girls started walking down the sidewalk toward Kress with Danielle merrily walking in the middle holding their hands. Kress was primarily a clothes, shoes, and accessories store with a men's, women's, and children's department. Their Aunt Nicky worked in the women's department.

"Let's go to the children's department," Laura said as she steered Danielle in that direction.

After almost an hour of awing over all the pretty summer clothes, Danielle finally picked out a red-and-blue short set outfit and a bright yellow sundress with little white flowers. Sydney held up the outfits against the little girl while she let her look in the store mirror. The sundress was very cute, and she could wear it to church.

"Hey, they might have some cute hair ribbons over in children's accessories; let's walk over to that aisle," Laura suggested.

Another thirty minutes later of "oh, these are so pretty," Danielle settled on some red hairbows that had red, white, and blue ribbon connected to them. The lil girl informed the two teens that she already had some yellow ribbons and barrettes at home to match her new sundress. Laura and Sydney laughed at the little fashionista.

They were walking toward the store checkout when Laura heard a familiar voice.

"Hey, girls, I didn't know you were coming down to Main Street today," Aunt Nicky greeted them.

"I've got new clothes and hair ribbons," Danielle announced with a big smile, holding up her new clothes.

"I see! Let me take them for you, and I'll ring them up later with my employee discount and bring them to you tomorrow," Aunt Nicky announced.

Danielle's face immediately dropped. Laura knew her lil sis was excited to carry her new purchases home.

"Auntie, that's OK, they're already on summer sale with big markdowns," Laura spoke up.

"Yes, we got some good sales going on now that the July 4th holiday has passed. We're gearing up for fall and back-to-school shopping. Don't you girls go buying no school clothes out of here without letting me know so that I can get them on discount," Aunt Nicky continued.

"OK," Laura and Sydney responded simultaneously.

"All right, I'll see you all tomorrow and don't go spending that tobacco money all in one day!" she hollered out all loud, as she walked away toward the women's department.

"Your auntie is so funny," Sydney commented. "But maybe she can get us a good discount on a couple of fall jackets or a winter coat."

Laura changed the subject as they got in line to pay for Danielle's clothes. She had more than enough Kress clothes in her closet already.

By the time they checked out, it was almost 2:30 p.m., so the girls decided to walk down to Mae's Grill. As they settled into a window booth, Laura saw Mike and Amy stroll pass the window. The two girls exchanged a few comments about Mike and Amy's seemingly budding friendship and speculated that they were probably on their way to the 3:00 p.m. matinee.

Listening to the teens, Danielle asked, "Laura, What's a mat… matinee? Can we go?"

"It's a name for an early movie, and no, we can't go today. Maybe another Saturday before school starts," her sister replied and then asked, "What do you want for lunch?"

"A chocolate milkshake," the lil girl proudly announced.

Laura and Sydney fell into laughter at her excitement. Danielle entertained them all through lunch.

Laura was keeping an eye on the time as they left the grill; it was about 3:20 and she wanted to make sure they caught the 4:00 p.m. bus home.

"Oh, let's go in here," Sydney said as they approached one of the young adult clothing stores that had not moved out to the mall.

Danielle was mesmerized by the bejeweled and sparkly decorated t-shirts. Her enthusiasm led to Laura and Sydney purchasing two t-shirts each to wear with their new jeans. The girls got to the transfer station just in time to catch the 4:00 p.m. bus. Danielle clutched her shopping bag to her chest as she watched the cars go by from the bus window. Everybody's stride was a little slower as they walked down the hill from the bus stop. Laura carried Danielle's shopping bag in one hand while the lil girl walked in the middle holding her and Sydney's hand. As they walked past the school playground, Danielle did not pester Laura to let her go and play on the swings.

"I think that large chocolate milkshake has someone a little tired," Sydney teased.

The teen girls continued chatting about clothes and starting high school until they came to the street intersection turnoff point. Laura reminded Sydney to save the Sunday ads, especially the Sears flyer. The teens were planning to get together on Sunday and review the ads.

"Bye, squirt," Sydney said to Danielle as she jokingly pulled her ponytail.

Laura and Danielle walked toward their house hand in hand. The lil girl did not take off running because all the walking, burger, fries, and chocolate milkshake had definitely slowed her down.

It was Sunday night already. Why did Saturday and Sunday have to go by so fast? Laura pondered as she laid her work clothes out for Monday morning, the start of week four on the tobacco farm. After Sunday dinner, Laura had gone to Sydney's house to look at the sales ad. There were a lot of sales on summer clothes. After looking through the clothes advertisements, she scoured through the Sears hardware and appliance flyer. There it was—a Kenmore dryer for $229. It was more than a week's pay on the tobacco farm. Laura had folded the flyer and put it in her pocket while at Sydney's house. Getting ready for bed, she took the flyer out of her pocket and placed it in her money envelope. Counting her money, she had only spent $23 on Saturday, so she had $357. Oh, but I do need to give John some money for more sandwich meat, Laura remembered as she took a five-dollar bill out of her money envelope.

A WHOLE MONTH

"Can y'all believe today starts our fourth week working on the tobacco farm? Come Friday it will be a whole month!" Laura said to the group as they waited for Mr. Isaiah and Mr. Nate to pull up.

"Ah, yeah," Jacob and Mike responded simultaneously.

"Y'all girls be under the shelter while we are out in the sun loading them tobacco trucks all day," Jacob said.

Even though they wore baseball caps, the guys still had some deep tans, Laura observed. They looked good, but not nearly as handsome as Daniel, she mused.

"Y'all are old enough for work permits, so why didn't you get regular summer jobs?" Laura asked.

"I didn't want to work in fast food," Jacob responded.

"And I'd rather be outside than working fast food too," Mike agreed.

"Besides I don't think my mom and dad would have agreed to Sydney working out in the country on the tobacco farm without me," Jacob added. "Right, squirt?" he teased his sister.

"Yeah right, he's my protector," Sydney teased him back even though she knew he was right.

"Well, we wouldn't have summer jobs if it wasn't for the tobacco farm," Amy chimed in. "So, I'm glad you guys decided not to work fast food."

"And even though these are some long, hot days, we're making more money than part-time fast-food work with our cash paydays on Fridays," Laura added.

"Oh yeah!" they all said and laughed as Mr. Isaiah pulled up right on time, at 7:00 a.m.

The workweek had become pretty routine for the young teen crew. Their camaraderie was growing with their new country friends. The lunchtime conversations were filled with lots of good-natured joking. Laura really liked getting in a few minutes of one-on-one conversation with Daniel each day. Ever since Mr. David Sr. had left the extra folding chairs for the teens to use, Daniel had sat beside her every day.

The workweek was progressing swiftly without any glitches, then came Thursday afternoon. The city teen crew had loaded up into the cargo bed of Mr. Isaiah's truck for the ride home. A gentle rain started to fall as soon as Mr. Isaiah turned off the dirt road onto the paved two-lane highway.

"Oh boy, I hope we make it home before it really starts to rain," Laura said.

"I hope we're riding away from the storm," Sydney chimed in.

About that time a streak of lightning flashed in the sky. Everybody sat up! The rain picked up slightly and another streak of lightning danced in the sky. They had only been on the road a few minutes. Suddenly, Mr. Isaiah made a wide U-turn on the two-lane paved road and was driving faster, headed in the opposite direction away from Ervinsville! The teens were starting to get wet with the wind blowing the rain back into the truck.

"He must be taking us back to the tobacco barn," Jacob spoke up.

But as soon as Jacob spoke, Mr. Isaiah drove right past the turn-off to the barns and continued straight. A couple of miles down the road, he made a right turn onto a very long gravel road. Then, like out of nowhere, this large red brick house appeared. It was two stories and had a huge white porch that looked like it circled the whole house.

"Wow!" Laura said out loud.

The house had a circular paved driveway that branched off to the right and to the left. Mr. Isaiah drove straight toward the house and veered to the right. He pulled up close to the porch.

"Hurry up, kids, get up on that porch!" His voice boomed at them from the truck's cab.

The teens quickly jumped out of the truck and ran up onto the porch. Mr. Isaiah drove toward the back of the house. They walked around the circular porch to see where he had gone. Mr. Isaiah parked the truck under this huge covered overhang. Attached to the overhang was a covered walkway that went right up to the backside of the porch. Laura had never seen anything like it! This must be a mansion, she thought.

Mr. Isaiah jumped up on the porch and announced, "We're going to wait a few minutes to see if this storm passes. I don't think we could have made it to Ervinsville without you young folks getting drenched. That lightning was far off, but it's better to be safe."

He walked around to where he had initially let them out of the truck and offered the teens some seats on the porch while he went inside to find his wife. Laura noticed that Mr. Isaiah took off his work boots and left them on the porch. The porch was gigantic and circled the whole house. It had a lot of depth and was completely covered by a roof, so they were no longer getting wet. Laura looked around. There was a porch swing and plenty of chairs. But no one took a seat.

They all just stood there, huddled together on the porch. The teens were probably all thinking the same thing; they were too wet and dirty to sit on those nice cushioned chairs.

"I hope this rain stops soon," Sydney spoke up.

The rain wasn't heavy but enough for them to get pretty wet during the ride home. Mr. Isaiah came outside and updated them on the situation. He had called Mr. Wilson and told him that they were at his house waiting for the rain to let up. He had also called

Mr. Nate to come and take some of them home in the cab of his truck if the rain didn't let up in the next few minutes.

Laura pulled her watch out of her pants pocket and glanced at it. It was already almost 6:00 p.m., the time they usually got home. If they didn't leave soon, she would have to ask to use the phone to call Grandma Annie.

"Isaiah, Roy is on the phone for you," a woman's voice announced from behind the sightly open door.

That must be Mrs. Dorothy, his wife, Laura concluded. Mr. Isaiah went inside and closed the door behind himself.

"Have you ever talked to Mrs. Dorothy?" Laura whispered to Sydney.

"No, not really. I've seen my mom talking to her at church." Sydney shrugged her shoulders.

The rain stopped, and the sun came out blazing as if the almost thirty-minute rain shower had never even happened. They all saw a familiar large black truck coming around the circular driveway.

"Come on, young folks, let's roll!" Mr. Isaiah bellowed as he came back out onto the porch. He pushed a cushion to the side and sat down in one of the rocking chairs to put his work boots back on.

"Hey, Nate, you want to ride with me to get these young folks home before its time to pick them up again?" he laughed good-heartedly.

As they were getting into the truck, Laura heard Mr. Isaiah updating Mr. Nate. Mr. Roy Smith had called. He and Mrs. Mary were checking to see if he had made it to the city with the young folks since the rainstorm came up so quickly.

The cargo bed of the truck was already dry, as if no rain had even fallen. That little bit of rain had left a hot, humid thickness in the air. The teen crew all leaned back in the truck, taking in the slight breeze as they finally headed back toward Ervinsville. Laura wondered why Mrs. Dorothy never came outside. Maybe she was just shy or maybe the sight of us about scared the woman to near death. Laura laughed, looking around the back of the truck. They were a wet, dirty, frightful sight. Their already-dirty clothes had gotten wet again, then redried from the heat.

By the time the truck pulled up in front of Sydney's house, Laura felt like she was wearing a ton of dirty bricks. Everything felt heavy. It was a little after seven o'clock, and both Mr. and Mrs. Wilson were waiting on the front porch.

"Sorry to get your youngins home so late; we had to wait out that little storm," Mr. Nate shouted from the passenger side of the truck's cab.

"No problem, as long as everybody's safe," Mr. Wilson said while walking down the porch steps to greet the young crew.

"OK, see y'all tomorrow morning," Mr. Isaiah bellowed as he drove off.

He never turned the engine off. Mr. Isaiah was always so punctual; the rain delay must have thrown off his whole evening. It didn't even look like a drop of rain had fallen in their neighborhood. The street was bone dry. Everybody was ready for the extra-long workday to end.

Grandma Annie and Danielle were also waiting for Laura on the porch.

"I figured you all got held up by the weather," her grandma greeted Laura as she reached the porch. Grandma Annie continued, "I could see lightning in the distance, but we didn't get a drop of rain."

Standing at the bottom of the porch steps, Laura explained their afternoon storm experience to her grandma and Danielle. Looking up at their porch, it seemed really small to Laura after seeing Mr. Isaiah's porch that circled his whole house. There was no way Laura could walk up those steps today; she waited for her lil sis to come down the steps.

Laura did not even remember falling asleep. She was still in Danielle's bed with her lil sis snuggled up against her when the alarm clock went off. Laura just barely recalled coaxing Danielle to read to her for a change. What a day Thursday had turned out to be, she thought as she quietly slipped out of the twin bed.

"Yes, payday Friday!" Laura said to her reflection in the bathroom mirror with a big smile.

The morning porch conversation was all about getting caught in Thursday's storm in the country and how not a drop of rain came down in the city, even though it was only about thirty miles distance. The girls chatted about how beautiful Mr. Isaiah's house was from the outside and speculated about how gorgeous it must be on the inside. Laura absolutely loved that big circular porch. She had never seen anything like it before, not even in the movies.

Laura asked Sydney, "Does Mr. Isaiah have any children?"

"I don't think so, at least I've never seen them with children at church," Sydney responded.

Just as Sydney was finishing her sentence, they saw the big, glistening black truck turn the corner.

"Happy Friday, young folks!" Mr. Isaiah and Mr. Nate shouted out to them.

Mr. Nate must be getting used to the teens because normally he just nodded his head, or maybe he was also very happy that it was Friday.

As the teens started climbing into the back of the truck, Amy commented, "I bet this is getting ready to be a very wet tobacco kinda Friday."

They all groaned.

The first truckload of tobacco was not too wet because it was the load that was left under the overhang Thursday evening. But that second and third truckload, oh my goodness, Laura thought as those wet tobacco leaves kept hitting her in the face and upper body each time she grabbed and strung a bundle for looping. Their upper bodies were getting drenched with wetness and dirt from the tobacco leaves, even though the sun was beaming outside the overhang. There was not one cloud in the sky.

From the women's morning conversation, the girls found out that all of them had gotten home just before the sky opened up with the downpour of rain. None of the women had thought Mr. Isaiah had enough time to get the teens home, especially when they had seen the lightning dancing in the sky. And just like that, in about thirty minutes, the sky was just as blue and clear as ever.

"Yep," the women and teen girls said in agreement.

"Here comes the fellas, let's rinse off some of this dirt," Mrs. Mary announced.

The women were never as dirty as Laura and the girls, but today they all did a quick dash to the outhouse.

"Hi, Laura, I was glad to hear that y'all made it home safely last night," Daniel said as he walked up to greet her before getting the folding chairs.

"Thanks, we waited out the storm at Mr. Isaiah's house," she responded, touching her bandanna to make sure all her hair was tucked underneath.

"Yeah, Jacob and Mike told us about it," he continued the conversation as they walked toward the barn. "These little summer evening storms don't last long. I just hope the weekend is not another washout."

They carried their chairs and lunches out to the big, welcoming tree. As they were sitting down under the teen lunch tree, Mrs. Cindy came over and spoke up, saying, "I know y'all got home really late yesterday, so I fried up a big batch of chicken legs to go with them chips you young people be eating."

Laura glanced at Daniel and David Jr.; they had big grins on their faces as their mom talked. She remembered Daniel telling her that his mom was a really good cook. Mrs. Cindy gave them each foil paper with two big chicken legs wrapped inside. Laura's mouth was salivating because she usually only got fried chicken on

Sundays. This was really a treat! Everything went quiet as everybody thoroughly enjoyed their freshly fried chicken legs.

"Those chicken legs were delicious; your mom is a great cook," Laura said to Daniel as they began their quick cleanup of the lunch area.

She wasn't just being flattering, Laura really meant it. She wanted a foil package of chicken to take home for later but didn't want to look too greedy in front of Daniel, so she kept quiet and didn't ask for seconds.

Everybody was glad to see that fifth truck swap out because they knew it was the last truck for the week. You would think it had rained all night as wet as each load of tobacco had been. Mr. Isaiah and the others must have had the same sentiment, because the three trucks came in from the fields a little earlier, at exactly 5:00 p.m. They had just a little more tobacco to finish stringing while the guys loaded up their lunch coolers into their trucks.

While giving the girls their pay envelopes, Mr. Isaiah told them he had brought some watermelons from his garden for their families to enjoy this weekend. He really appreciated their positive attitudes about yesterday's weather calamity.

"Thanks, it wasn't too bad!" all three teen girls said in unison with big smiles.

Mr. Isaiah was really a kind man, Laura mused as she folded her envelope in half and put it in her pocket. She patted her pocket for reassurance, as she had done every Friday.

As everyone was saying their goodbyes, Daniel walked up to Laura and quietly asked, "Can you write your phone number on a piece of paper and bring it for me on Monday?"

"Sure" was all Laura could stammer out as her brain went instantly into awestruck mode.

"OK, thanks, have a good weekend, see you Monday," Daniel said all in one breath before turning to run toward his family's truck.

"Laura, come on," Sydney said, bringing Laura out of her brain fog.

She couldn't wait to tell Sydney. As the truck headed toward the two-lane paved road, Laura leaned over to Sydney and whispered, "Daniel asked for my phone number."

"I knew he liked you," Sydney declared.

Laura shushed Sydney with a look and shake of her head. "We'll talk later," she said, not wanting Amy or the guys to know that Daniel had asked for her number.

Mr. Isaiah dropped a watermelon off to Mrs. Wilson. Instead of giving the teens a watermelon to carry home, he then drove each one of the teens to their house to deliver the watermelons. They were very grateful because those watermelons were definitely too big to carry down the street. Especially after a day of standing with outstretched arms stringing tobacco, Laura thought as she thanked Mr. Isaiah. He moved swiftly, placing the watermelon on the porch and was gone before her grandma even came outside.

"Hey, Grandma, Mr. Isaiah gave us a watermelon out of his garden," Laura exclaimed.

"Hi, baby, that's a nice big watermelon; I sure hope it's sweet," Grandma Annie said, peering over the top of her glasses.

"I'm sure it is because he brought some for us at lunch one Friday, and it was sweet," she assured her grandma as she sat down to take off her filthy sneakers to take the watermelon into the kitchen.

"That little Danielle is going to want some watermelon right now," Grandma Annie said and laughed.

And sure enough, there she was at the screen door, eyeing the watermelon. Danielle held the screen door open for Laura. Her grandma was right because her lil sis was starting to go into tantrum mode for watermelon. Thank goodness Grandma Annie firmly explained how she was going to slice the watermelon up and put it in the refrigerator so that it could get nice and cold for Saturday.

Danielle accepted the explanation and turned her attention to another subject.

"So today is payday Friday," the lil girl said matter-of-factly to Laura.

"Yes, it is!" Laura said, laughing at Danielle. She touched her pocket with one hand and took her lil sis's hand. They started their walk home.

STRATEGIC PLANNING WEEKEND

After four weeks of working on the tobacco farm, Laura had $512 saved up for shopping. She had already put the $40 in a separate envelope and placed it on her mama's bedside table. Laura had also given John another five dollars to get her some more lunch meat. There were no other obligations tied to her $512 other than school clothes shopping! She had two more weeks to work. Ever since almost spending her entire first pay on summer clothes, she and Sydney had been working on their shopping list. They used the Sunday ads to see which stores had the best sales. The teen girls had decided to go to the mall today, just to kinda scope out a few stores.

Interrupting Laura's thoughts, Danielle, peering at her from the other twin bed, asked, "Laura, can I go with you today?"

"No, I'm going out to the mall, and Mama said that you can't go that far on the bus. We'll go over to Grandma Annie's and get some watermelon when I get back," Laura appeased her.

"OK, I'm hungry," The lil girl responded as she got up to start the day.

Laura had been lying in bed mulling over her shopping strategy. She got up to go fix Danielle some breakfast and to wash her work clothes. She wanted to get the laundry done before going to the mall.

Laura only brought $40 with her because she didn't want to be tempted to spend more money. Sydney met her at the corner intersection, and they walked to the bus stop talking about their favorite subjects, clothes and boys.

"Maybe the storm on Thursday and not knowing if you got home safely prompted Daniel to ask for your phone number," Sydney stated.

"Girl, if it did, thank you for the little rainstorm," Laura responded.

Both girls burst into laughter as they reached the end of the street and started up the hill.

It was a beautiful Saturday, and Laura loved being out and about. She gazed out the bus window at the cars whizzing past. When their bus pulled into the transfer station, Sydney tugged on Laura's arm, hurrying her to the 11:30 a.m. bus to the mall. The mall was buzzing with lots of people. Probably because it was the first weekend in August and everybody's thoughts were turning toward school reopening. The teen girls strolled through the mall, stopping periodically to check out the clothes in a few stores. They also saw some friends from junior high and stopped to chat. Excitement was in the air. Laura and Sydney strolled through the Sears clothing department. Both teens thought the clothes either looked too childish or too old-fashioned. Definitely not the high school look they wanted.

"Let's go check out the appliance section," Laura said.

"Appliances?" Sydney said with curiosity as they walked toward the back of Sears.

"Yeah, I want to try and convince my mom to get a clothes dryer. At least for use during the winter. Girl, I be bringing in frozen cold clothes from that clothesline," Laura explained.

"I know," Sydney responded. "We have a clothes dryer, but my mom hardly ever uses it. She said the clothes smell better and last longer if you hang them outside."

"That is exactly what Miss Elaine said. But we do the hanging, the bringing in, and the folding in that cold," Laura wittily retorted. "Oh, here they go." Laura motioned for Sydney to follow her.

The clothes dryers were running from between $220 to $250. Some of them were small and compact, and others were a little larger. Laura thought the small compact one would fit perfectly in the corner in their kitchen.

Walking up to them, the salesman asked, "Can I help you, young ladies?"

"No, sir, we're just looking," Laura responded.

"Well, we have some great sales going on; let me know if you young ladies need help or have any questions," the salesman stated and walked away.

The teens lightly giggled as they turned to walk away. Rarely were they referred to as young ladies, it sounded so grown up. Laura was contemplating how to go about reapproaching her mama about buying a clothes dryer.

The girls were getting hungry and decided to walk down to the food court and get some lunch. Settling into one of the small tables with their drinks, burgers, and fries, they both heard the familiar voices at the same time.

"Hey, you two out here spending your tobacco money?" Carolyn said, approaching their table with Brenda.

"Maybe you all should come down to K's and spend some of that tobacco money. We got some good sales going on," Brenda added.

"Maybe we will," Sydney responded.

Laura took a bite of her burger.

"Oh, there's Debra and Wanda, let's go sit with them," Carolyn said to Brenda.

"See you two later, tell your brothers we said hi," Brenda added as they walked away in a fit of gaiety to bother somebody else.

"Maybe we should check out K's; they do carry some nice teen clothes," Sydney commented.

"Yeah, on a day they're off from work." Laura laughed as she took another bite of her burger. The girls finished eating and decided to take the next bus back downtown to Main Street.

The bus from the mall got the teens downtown to the transfer station just in time to catch the 4:00 p.m. bus home. Thank goodness the bus wasn't crowded. Reaching their stop, the girls exited and began their leisurely walk down the hill talking about their shopping plans.

"Hey." Another familiar voice shouted to the teens as they walked past the school playground. It was Eric running toward them.

"Hey, you all just missed a game. We got enough time to play another one; why don't you all stop and watch the game," Eric greeted them.

"Not me," Laura responded. "I promised Danielle that I would take her to my grandma's for watermelon."

"Watermelon sounds good," Sydney added.

Laura looked at Sydney sideways knowing full well that she had a watermelon too.

"It sure does; give me a few minutes and I'll catch up with you instead of playing the second game," Eric stated as he turned and ran back toward the field.

"Girl, did he just invite himself to my grandma's house for watermelon?" Laura said and laughed heartily. She continued, "I told you that he likes you, and you know that you got plenty of watermelon at home talking about it sounds good."

Both girls laughed and continued their conversation as they walked toward Grandma Annie's house. And sure enough, Eric had caught up with Laura and Sydney by the time they got to the corner intersection. Laura went to quickly get Danielle. Eric and Sydney continued walking down the street to Laura's grandma's house.

The group had a good time laughing, talking, and eating watermelon on Grandma Annie's porch. She was always hospitable to the neighborhood kids, and Sydney was practically a member of the family. Danielle also entertained them with her antics and questions. Their conversation flowed because they had all pretty much grown up in the neighborhood together. Eric told them that in addition to playing softball, he was also thinking about trying out for the basketball team this year. Laura knew her grandma was keeping an eye on Eric. She was probably trying to figure out which of the girls he liked since he chose to hang out with them on a beautiful, sunny Saturday afternoon instead of being out somewhere playing ball.

"OK, young people, it's time to clean up; put those watermelon rinds in this trash bag. I don't want no flies all over my porch," Grandma Annie instructed them.

The teens started cleaning up the area.

"Mrs. Annie, thanks for the watermelon," Eric said as he took the trash bag and put it in the large outside garbage can.

"Thanks, Grandma, we're also leaving. Danielle and I have to bring in some clothes from the line before it gets dark," Laura explained.

The three teens and Danielle headed up the sidewalk. When they got to the corner intersection, Laura and her lil sis turned right to go home, and Eric and Sydney continued straight toward Sydney's house. It had been a really good Saturday, except for those two lines of laundry that still needed to be brought in and folded, Laura thought.

"Come on, Danielle, I'll race you to the clothesline!" Laura shouted.

The sweltering heat hit them as they opened the front door to catch the church bus. Laura always thought August was the hottest month of the summer, and this first Sunday in August was proving her right. Danielle looked so cute in her yellow sundress with those matching barrettes swinging in the air as she ran toward the church bus. John had not even come outside yet. Grandma Annie and Deacon Harris were going to be upset if he made everybody late for church service. By the time Laura reached the church bus door, John came out the front door walking slow. It's so hot; Laura assumed that was why her brother was moving so slow today. Besides, they all knew that first Sunday services were always a little longer than the regular services.

When church service was over, Laura, Danielle, and a couple of other bus riders were standing under a tree on the church grounds waiting for Deacon Harris to come out and start up the bus. The bus door was open, but no one wanted to sit on that hot bus waiting for him to come out of the church. Laura saw John standing up near the church entrance talking to Angie Brown. Probably making Sunday afternoon plans, she discerned. Sydney had called last night and told Laura that as she and Eric were walking up the street, her brother, Jacob, was coming down the opposite end of the street about the same time. He and Eric talked softball for a few minutes, then Eric continued on his way.

"Come on, folks, let's load up," Deacon Harris shouted as he walked toward the church bus.

He could have at least let the air conditioner run for a few minutes before loading up, Laura sighed as she got on the hot church bus. She wished they could just get off at Grandma Annie's house instead of having to go home then walk in the heat back over there for dinner. Oh well, at least she could change into some shorts.

Sunday dinner was always the most scrumptious meal of the week. Her mama had fried up a big batch of chicken wings while they were at church. Laura thought about Friday as she fixed her plate. A big, fat chicken leg from Mrs. Cindy would go real good with two of her mama's chicken wings and this potato salad. Everybody was enjoying the meal.

As they were eating, Laura casually asked her grandma, "How often do you use your clothes dryer?"

Her mama gave her an instantaneous side-eye look.

"Not too much, I still like to hang my clothes outside except for my unmentionables," Grandma Annie answered.

"Unmen…unmentionables! What are those?" Danielle asked.

John just looked down and concentrated on his plate of food.

"My undies, child." Grandma laughed.

"Grandma, we're eating!" John exclaimed incredulously.

All the women and girls had a good laugh. Laura's mama interjected with slight agitation about Laura trying to get her to buy a clothes dryer. She reminded her own mom that they didn't have a clothes dryer when they were coming up. Her mom had gotten it much later in life after arthritis had made it too hard for her to carry clothes outside.

"Most people only use them during the winter when it's too rainy or cold to hang clothes outside," Laura said as she stood up to take her plate to the sink.

"Use them what?" Aunt Nicky asked as she came into house, dropping her purse onto the couch.

Grandma really needs to start locking that screen door, Laura thought.

"Laura wants me to get a clothes dryer," her mama explained.

"Oh, well, have her buy one with that tobacco money," Aunt Nicky retorted while starting to fix a plate of food.

That's just what I might do, Laura muttered to herself. "Mama, can Danielle and I go home? It's too hot for her to play outside today," Laura asked.

"Wow, talk about spending that tobacco money and she is ready to go," Aunt Nicky teased Laura.

"Yeah, I've got to head out too," John said as he stood up to take his and Danielle's plates to the sink.

"I made some fruit cups with the rest of that watermelon, look in the refrigerator," Grandma Annie announced.

Laura opened the refrigerator and saw the tray of paper cups filled with watermelon and cantaloupe cut in cubes with a few grapes covered in plastic wrap. The fruit cups looked inviting, but Laura was not about to stick around to be the center of conversation while she ate a fruit cup. She took a plastic bag from the cupboard and put six fruit cups in it for her, John, and Danielle.

Their mama was going to stay awhile and talk to Grandma and Aunt Nicky. John headed up the street while Laura and Danielle went home.

The girls settled on the couch watching television and enjoying their fruit cups. Laura had intended to sit with her lil sis for a few minutes and enjoy the nice cool living room air. The big window unit air conditioner slightly cooled the whole house, but the living room was always the coolest. Those few minutes were almost an hour later when she woke up with Danielle snuggled up against her on the couch. The house was peaceful with just the sound of the television and the hum of the air conditioner. Only two more weeks to work on the tobacco farm, Laura pondered. Her thoughts started to race with all the things she wanted to get done before school started. The phone rang, interrupting her thoughts and waking Danielle.

"Hey, girl, isn't it super-hot today?" Sydney greeted her.

ON THE DOWNSLOPE

Laura touched her jeans pocket as she walked up to Sydney's porch and greeted the crew. She was double-checking, even though she knew the index card with her name and phone number neatly printed was folded in quarters in her pocket. Laura had just placed it there less than five minutes ago. Sunday night before going to bed, she had carefully printed her information on the card. First, she had written the phone number on regular writing paper but then decided to use one of the index cards left over from school, because working in the tobacco was always damp, especially on Mondays. Laura didn't want her phone number to smear.

At precisely 7:00 a.m., Mr. Isaiah pulled up. Mr. Nate was back to his morning nod. The teen crew climbed into the back of the cargo bed of the truck to start their fifth week on the tobacco farm. They headed out to the country with Mr. Wilson standing morning watch on the porch to ensure the young teens were safely on their way to the tobacco farm.

During the ride out to the farm, Jacob told the group about Mr. Isaiah giving away a bunch of watermelons at their church yesterday. He had done the same thing for the July 4th holiday.

"He must have a large garden on land somewhere else in the country because I didn't see one in his backyard when we were at his house last Thursday," Laura commented.

"My mom said his family has a lot of land out here," Sydney informed the group.

Either Mr. Isaiah was driving faster or they had really gotten used to the ride because it seemed like they were only in the back of the truck for about ten to fifteen minutes.

"Good morning, Mary. We're on the two-week harvest countdown!" Mr. Isaiah bellowed from the cab without turning off the truck.

"I know that's right, it's gonna be a busy week!" Mrs. Mary shouted back while walking toward the truck to greet the young crew. "We got two weeks to finish turning these youngins into country folks," she teased with a hearty laugh as Mr. Isaiah turned the truck around and was gone to the fields.

Laura looked at Mrs. Mary, Mrs. Cindy, and Miss Elaine standing there in their bib overalls, long-sleeve t-shirts, and bandannas. They were not bad-looking women, but their faces were plain, no makeup, not even a pair of stud earrings. Surely, they did not dress like this on the weekends. No way, Laura thought as she got into her stringing position beside Mrs. Mary.

During their first break, Sydney asked Laura if she had remembered to write down her phone number for Daniel. Subconsciously touching her pocket, Laura told Sydney that she had her watch in one pocket and an index card folded up with her phone number in the other pocket. Laura still brought her watch to the farm every day even though she rarely had to check it, she knew the time of day by the rotation of the tobacco trucks.

The teen girls were maintaining their rhythmic pace as they worked through the second then the third load of tobacco. Laura knew that in about two hours it would be time for their lunch break. The morning was moving right along. The emptier the third truck got, the more Laura's thoughts became preoccupied with how she could give Daniel the index card without bringing a lot of attention to them. She didn't want to just hand it to him in front of everybody. Hopefully, they would get a brief moment without any eyes on them.

The guys were moving a little slow when they came in for lunch. According to the guys, Mondays were the worst for harvesting and loading the trucks. Daniel smiled as he walked up to greet Laura. To Laura, he had the most mesmerizingly dimpled smile that she had ever seen. Not surprisingly, everybody had some version of a fresh fruit cup for lunch.

"That was really nice of Mr. Isaiah to give us those watermelons; they were really sweet," Laura said to Daniel.

"Yeah, they were pretty good. My mom also has one row of watermelons in our garden; they're good too. Mr. Isaiah's farm is pretty big; he sells his watermelons and some other vegetables to the local grocery stores in the surrounding towns throughout the county," Daniel explained.

"Oh, wow, my brother works part-time at the local grocery store near our neighborhood. I bet he's stocked some of Mr. Isaiah's watermelons," she said with laughter in her voice.

"Probably, because you know Ervinsville and Herd are in the same county," Daniel informed her. "Herd sits just barely inside the Vernon County line; we play your high school at least once during softball, football, and basketball seasons."

"Really, I didn't know that," Laura responded. Hmm…Laura pondered as she took a bite from her fruit cup.

"We've got our last rec league softball games this weekend," Anthony announced to the group of teens.

"And then next week high school football practice starts!" David Jr. added with a pump up and down of his arm. "I'm ready to get back out on that football field for my last season."

And just like that, all the guys were engrossed in discussing the upcoming professional football season and their favorite teams.

Sydney was sitting on Laura's left side and leaned over and whispered in Laura's ear, "Have you given Daniel your number yet?"

Laura shook her head no.

"OK, young folks, let's get this Monday done!" Mr. Roy shouted to the teens.

Laura had noticed that Mrs. Mary and Mr. Roy were the natural leaders of the group. One of the two of them always roused the teens to get moving toward the end of the lunch break. They had also called Mr. Isaiah last week to check on the teen crew during the rainstorm. Everybody started to gather their lunch containers and folding chairs.

While picking up Laura's chair and folding it, Daniel leaned inward toward her and softly asked, "Did you remember to write your number down for me?"

Laura smiled and responded, "Yes," as she took the index card out of her jeans pocket and quickly placed it in his open hand.

Daniel closed his hand and swiftly placed his closed hand into his overall pocket. It happened in a matter of seconds, so Laura was pretty sure nobody saw them, except maybe Sydney. Even though their hands had barely touched, Laura's heart was racing in her chest. For the rest of the day, all she could think about was whether or not Daniel would call her that night.

With aching arms and legs, they all just leaned back in the truck and enjoyed the breezy ride home. Their young bodies always felt the effects of tobacco farm work, especially on Monday afternoons.

As they entered the city limit, Sydney whispered to Laura, "Girl, I saw Daniel talking and then you reaching out to him when we were cleaning up the lunch area. Did you give him the card?"

"Yes," Laura said and fidgeted a little, hoping no one else saw the brief exchange.

Especially Jacob and Mike because they played ball with her brother. Mr. Isaiah rounded the curve and there was Mrs. Wilson posted on the porch. She was a welcoming sight, signaling the end of the workday.

Monday's dinner was always leftovers from Sunday, but Laura had taken a couple of the chicken wings and a fruit cup for lunch. She really didn't want it again for dinner. After showering and changing into her pajamas, she decided on a bowl of Frosted Flakes cereal for dinner. Of course, Danielle insisted on having the same thing. Laura was sitting on the couch going through the sales papers that she had gotten from Sydney. The Kress store actually had a good sale on winter coats. Laura was mulling over at least getting her winter coat from Kress, but not any school clothes. She really wanted to start high school with a different look. Just about everything in her closet was from Kress and had been altered to fit her. Nope, she wanted new school clothes.

Just as Laura was getting Danielle settled into bed, the phone rang. She rushed down the hallway to answer it before the ringing stopped.

"Hello," she answered.

"Hello, may I speak to Laura," the deep, melodious voice greeted her. Laura instantly recognized Daniel's voice.

"Hi, it's me," she answered in almost a hushed whisper.

"I hope it's not too late to call. I had softball practice this afternoon since we have our final games this weekend, but I wanted to give you a quick call to see if you gave me the right phone number," Daniel said jokingly.

Laura could just see his eyes laughing at her with those dimples dancing in his cheeks. She laughed back and said, "I was just hoping the card didn't get wet, so you could read the numbers."

"Oh, I got it memorized now," he responded.

Laura heard a voice calling him in the background; it sounded like Mrs. Cindy.

"I've got to go. I'll see you tomorrow. Good night," Daniel said all in one breath.

Their conversation was over as quickly as it began. But it didn't matter because Laura was enchanted by his voice. It sounded even deeper over the phone. She realized that she was still holding the phone handle and placed it back in its cradle. Even though the conversation was brief, Laura walked back down the hallway as if her bare feet were touching a cloud instead of the carpet. Danielle was already asleep snuggled up with her Scooby-Doo stuffed dog.

Laura lay on her bed imagining what a date with Daniel would be like. She had actually never been on a date, and Daniel was the first boy to call their house to talk to her. Laura drifted off to sleep, looking forward to Tuesday on the tobacco farm.

Everyone was moving about in a familiar groove. Workweek five was flowing as the end of tobacco harvest neared. The guys' lunchtime conversations were preoccupied with their upcoming busy softball weekend. But Daniel always made time to talk to Laura.

From the guys' conversation, Laura learned that her brother John, Jacob, and Mike also had final softball games this weekend. With them both working summer jobs on different schedules, she had just barely seen or even talked to her brother this summer. The park where the rec league teams played was a little further than the school playground but still within walking distance. Maybe she, Sydney, and their lil partner Danielle would walk down and watch a game on Saturday.

"I'm glad the softball season is ending so that I can have a couple of free weekends before school starts," Daniel said to Laura as they were finishing up Thursday's lunch.

"Yes, this summer has gone by really fast," Laura responded.

She must look a real sight to him with the bandanna tied around her head, dirty baggy jeans, and this dirty huge t-shirt, Laura thought as she reached up and touched her bandanna.

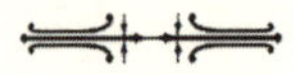

In what seemed like a blink of an eye, it was Friday! Laura grinned as the girls jumped out of the back of the truck to start their final workday of the week. The first truck was always strung fast because the women had it practically done by the time the teen girls arrived. Today, they finished stringing the second truckload a little early, which gave the teens a few extra minutes break while they waited for Mr. Nate to bring the third load.

"Hey, girl, have you talked to Daniel on the phone anymore since Monday night?" Sydney asked Laura as they got a small cup of water.

Of course, Laura had already told her best friend all about Monday night's phone call from Daniel.

"No," Laura answered. "But he's been getting home late because they've had extra softball practices for their final games this weekend."

"Girl, can you imagine having to go to softball practice after standing and stringing tobacco all day?" Sydney said with an incredulous look on her face.

Laura laughed and responded, "No way."

"What's going on?" Amy asked, walking up to them.

"We were just talking about the guys' final rec league games this weekend. Are you planning to go?" Laura asked.

"Yeah, I'll probably take my little brothers down to the park on Saturday; they love playing and watching softball," Amy responded.

"Cool, we're planning to come down and watch on Saturday also," Laura said.

"Oh, here comes Mr. Nate with truck three," Sydney announced.

The girls continued talking for a few more minutes while Mr. Nate switched out the trucks. Then they dropped their cups into the big trash can at the door of the barn and went to get back into stringing position under the overhang.

Mr. Isaiah and the three women had brought the teens a treat every Friday, so Laura really wasn't expecting anyone to bring anything today since it was week five and the tobacco harvest was coming to a close. Friday's lunch conversation was always upbeat about the coming weekend. Not to mention it was payday! Everybody was in a great mood.

Mrs. Mary, Mrs. Cindy, and Miss Elaine came walking over to the teen lunch tree carrying a smaller cooler. These three women are really something special, Laura smiled with genuine admiration as

Mrs. Mary started to pass out large paper cups filled to the brim with fresh cucumbers, tomatoes, red and yellow peppers, and some tiny macaroni marinated in some kind of dressing. Mrs. Mary explained that one of their favorite summer salads was a big bowl of pasta marinated with fresh vegetables from their garden. The cucumbers and tomatoes were from Mrs. Mary's garden, the peppers were from Mrs. Cindy's garden, and Miss Elaine made the homemade sauce using some of the herbs from her garden.

The guys wasted no time digging into their cups. Laura took a big forkful from her cup and put it in her mouth. All the taste buds in her mouth woke up! She couldn't believe how good the pasta salad tasted. She closed her eyes just savoring in all the flavors mixed with the slightly sweet vinaigrette.

"You really enjoying that pasta salad," Daniel said, observing her closed eyes. "I told you that my mom has a little garden. She loves working in it and cooking new stuff for us. My dad, David Jr., and me are her guinea pigs." He laughed.

Opening her eyes, Laura said, "Well, she must have practiced on y'all a lot because this salad is delicious."

She grinned at him and bit into another forkful of pasta. She could feel his eyes still watching her eat. Thoroughly enjoying the pasta salad, Laura thought, how do these women find time to do all this extra stuff in the evenings? Her grandma made an awesome potato salad. But Laura could only remember her making pasta salad a few times, and it was not this good.

"OK, young folks, don't let eating all that good pasta salad slow you down; we still got a full afternoon of work to do!" Mr. Roy shouted.

Mrs. Mary gave Mr. Roy a different medium size cooler to take back out to the field. That's just like her to make enough for the other guys, Laura and the girls surmised as they watched Mr. Roy put the cooler in the back of the truck with the guys.

"I'm going to ask Grandma Annie to bake something for everybody next week," Laura told Sydney as they walked toward the barn overhang. "Can you believe our six weeks are almost over?"

"Girl, finally," Sydney retorted. "I will miss the ladies though; they are really cool, and I know you're going to miss seeing Daniel," Sydney said teasingly to Laura.

Both girls laughed as they got back into stringing position, but Laura knew Sydney was right. She had really gotten used to talking and joking with Daniel every day. Yep, that part of working on the tobacco farm, she was surely going to miss.

The end of the Friday workday came just as quickly as it had started that morning. The three trucks came rolling down the dirt road, signaling the end of the fifth workweek. The usual goodbyes were flowing back and forth.

Daniel walked up to Laura with a smile and said, "I'll call you over the weekend." He winked, then dashed off to help his brother carry their stuff to the truck.

Laura just stood there watching him.

"Stop staring," Sydney said and nudged Laura, bringing her back to the task at hand.

The teen crew jumped into the cargo bed, ready to start the weekend. Laura patted her jeans pocket. Yep, another $200. Laura leaned back and enjoyed the breezy ride back to the city.

END OF SOFTBALL SEASON WEEKEND

The small wood frame house was quiet as the Saturday morning sunlight peeked through the bedroom window. The curtains blocked the direct sun from entering the bedroom. Laura had gotten used to getting up before dawn to work on the tobacco farm, but come Saturday mornings, she looked forward to those few extra hours lingering in bed. She laid there a few more minutes before getting up to start a load of laundry.

Laura and Sydney had talked on Friday night about their plans for Saturday. Their brothers were playing softball at 10:00 a.m. and then again at 2:00 p.m. Neither girl wanted to catch the first game but definitely the second game. She and Sydney had decided to walk down to the park around 11:30 a.m.

Laura was putting her work clothes in the washing machine when she heard her brother, John, up and moving around. He must be getting ready to go down to the park, she thought. Laura was sitting at the kitchen table eating her toast with strawberry jam, her favorite, when John walked in fully dressed in his softball uniform.

"Hey, sis, I haven't seen you all week," John greeted her as he grabbed a couple of apples from out of the bowl on the kitchen counter.

"Hey, we're planning to come down to the park and watch your 2:00 p.m. game," Laura greeted her brother.

"Yeah!" Danielle squealed as she came into the kitchen. She had heard Laura say they were going to the park.

"Cool," John responded. "We're playing on field number 8 for the 2:00 p.m. game."

"OK," Laura responded as she got a bowl out of the cabinet to fix Danielle a bowl of Frosted Flakes cereal.

Right about that time they heard a car horn. "Gotta go, see you at the park," John shouted as he headed to the front door.

Laura and Danielle followed him into the living room. Looking out the window, she saw that it was Mr. Wilson with Jacob, Mike, and Eric already in the car.

After eating breakfast, Danielle put on some jean shorts, a red top, and her blue sneakers. Laura clipped the red bows with the blue and red ribbon onto the top of each of her lil sis's ponytails. She looked very cute. It was going to be a hot day, so Laura also put a little visor cap on Danielle's head and pulled her ponytails out through the back. Laura sent her lil sis to watch some cartoons while she quickly hung out the load of clothes.

Putting on a pair of red hooped earrings to match her red tank top, Laura looked at her reflection in the mirror. She liked the way the earrings framed her face, especially with the deep tanned hue her face and arms had finally gotten during the past five weeks. The guys had deep tans after their first week on the tobacco farm. Every time she thought about the tobacco farm, Daniel's handsome, sun-kissed face popped into Laura's head. Still gazing into the mirror, Laura hoped his team won their games this weekend. Ah, one more week working on the tobacco farm, she sighed while brushing her hair back into a ponytail and putting on the sun visor. Ponytails had become her summer go-to hairstyle.

Danielle was anxious to get to the ballpark. But Laura knew her mama had more laundry to do, so she quickly went outside and brought in her dry work clothes. Coming in the back screen door, she saw her mama sitting at the kitchen table waiting for the coffee pot to perk. It was scorching hot outside. She didn't understand how her mama drank coffee during the summer. Laura had already left the envelope on her mama's night table with the $40 inside.

"Morning, Mama, we're going to the park to watch John's 2:00 p.m. game. It's their final weekend. Do you want to come with us?" Laura asked.

"No, it's too hot for me to be walking down to that park. John told me that he has a final makeup game tomorrow at 2:00 p.m. I was talking to your aunt, and we're going to drive down to the ballpark tomorrow and watch his final game, then come back to Mom's house for Sunday dinner." Her mama then added, "You and Danielle can come with us as soon as you get home from church tomorrow."

Taking the basket of work clothes and dumping them onto her twin bed, Laura muttered, "Just great," under her breath with a grimace. She did not want to spend her Saturday and Sunday at the ballpark.

Approaching the park, the girls could see that it was already crowded. There were multiple playing fields and people were everywhere. It was about 12:30 p.m. so they had plenty of time to walk around before the 2:00 p.m. game. Danielle wanted to run to the first play area she saw, but Laura held tightly to her hand. She explained that they would walk around a little first, then pick a play area close to field number 8. There were play areas scattered throughout the park. It had been a hot walk down to the ballpark so Sydney suggested they get some snow cones.

The girls munched on their snow cones as they meandered their way through the park, stopping periodically to greet some friends they hadn't seen all summer. Laura was not really a crowds person, but she was really enjoying being out and about in the park. Their whole summer had been a continuous rotation of sleep-tobacco farm-sleep.

"Girl, it's 1:30 p.m., we had better get to field number 8," Laura announced.

There was a play area near the ballfield, but Laura didn't want to let Danielle go play because it wasn't at an angle where she could watch the ball game and her lil sister at the same time. She convinced Danielle that it would be exciting to watch her big brother play softball first, then play afterward. Sydney's parents, Mr. and Mrs. Wilson, were already in the bleachers. The girls also saw Mike's dad and his younger brother and sister. Amy and her two little brothers were sitting a couple of rows behind Mike's family. Laura and Sydney decided to sit on the lower bleachers. She didn't want Danielle running up and down the bleacher stairs. They waved at everybody, and Sydney went up to speak to her parents.

"My dad has a cooler full of drinks, fruit, and snacks," Sydney said, handing them each a bottle of water. She continued, "He's been out here since early this morning."

Laura remembered that Mr. Wilson had picked up her brother, John. The softball game moved along at a steady pace. John was a good batter and runner. He scored a couple of home runs. Danielle was having a ball cheering and yelling for John. It was like their brother had his own little personal cheerleader.

Eric was a good catcher and covered second base. Jacob and Mike both played outfield. They had some great catches and stopped the other team from getting a few runs. Laura still couldn't understand how Jacob and Mike still wanted to play softball out in this heat after being out in the tobacco field all week. The sun was beaming extra bright. Guess they just love the game, she contemplated. She hoped Daniel and Anthony were having a good game day too.

The guys had already won their morning game and now had another victory! As soon as the game ended and before Laura could grab her hand, Danielle made a beeline straight through the crowd for her big brother. John picked her up and swung the lil girl around in the air. He was really happy that his sisters had come to watch him play. He picked Danielle up and swung her around again right as Angie walked up to congratulate him on the double wins.

"Are you all headed home?" John asked Laura.

"No, Sydney and I are going to take Danielle over to the play area and let her burn up some energy on the swings and slides," Laura answered him.

"OK, well I'm going to head home to shower and change. Then, I'm going to go hang out with some of the fellas from the team. So, don't stay down here too long and be careful walking home," he instructed Laura.

Angie and John walked off together. Sydney was talking to her parents and her brother, Jacob. Everybody was in a jovial mood about the two victories. Laura and Danielle walked over to congratulate Jacob and the other guys.

Swings, slides, and all sorts of climbing bars! Danielle had an absolute blast running from one to the other in the play area. The ribbons on the end of her bows were flying in the air but surprisingly still attached to her two ponytails. The lil girl had given her sun visor to Laura to hold because it was just in her way. Laura and Sydney sat on a park bench and watched Danielle run and play with the other kids while they ate a snack from Sydney's dad's cooler.

"My mom said that we're going to the early church service tomorrow so that we can come down and watch Jacob and them play their final game of the season; it's at 2:00 p.m." He gets to skip church and sleep in," Sydney explained. "Are y'all coming back down tomorrow?" she asked Laura.

"I don't know, Aunt Nicky and my mama are coming down to watch the game. I'll see what happens," Laura shrugged her shoulders. "Girl, did you see Carolyn eyeing my brother, John, after the game? But Angie was right there, Carolyn didn't stand a chance," Laura added with laughter in her voice.

Both of the teen girls broke out into a fit of laughter. After a full day of sun, softball, and playing in the park, Danielle was not quite as peppy for the walk home. The walk from the park was a little longer than their normal walk from the school playground. Laura and Sydney put her in the middle and held her hand, as usual, but walked at a much slower pace.

"Hey, did Daniel call you last night?" Sydney asked as they strolled down the street.

"No, but I sure hope they won their softball games today. I think they have games tomorrow also," Laura said and gestured with a flick in the air of her free hand.

"Bye, squirt. See y'all later," Sydney said as they reached the intersection.

Laura and Danielle waved goodbye as they continued down the street toward home.

"Who is Daniel?" Danielle asked Laura as they approached their house.

Oh, she tired but not too tired to hear every little word of my conversation with Sydney Laura laughed to herself.

"Just one of our friends from the tobacco farm," Laura responded nonchalantly.

Oh, her lil inquisitive sis must be really tired because that answer didn't generate any follow-up questions. Laura was happy with not having to answer any more questions about Daniel. The two sisters entered the house to the aroma of fried hamburgers. They sat at the kitchen table devouring the hamburgers and tater tots their mama had prepared. John had already been home and was gone out again. Laura looked out the kitchen window as she enjoyed her burger. The clothes were still hanging on the clothesline, swaying back and forth ever so likely as though they were calling her name. She already knew what her next task was going to be.

While Laura was outside taking down the clothes, her mama had Danielle take an early bath. By the time Laura was coming in with the third load of clothes, Danielle was sound asleep, curled up on the couch with her Scooby-Doo stuffed dog. Laura put the clothes basket down for a quick minute and took the phone off the little table, placing it on top of the clothes. Picking up the basket, she continued to the bedroom. Her mama briefly looked up from the television; she probably thought Laura was going to call Sydney.

Laura was actually hoping that Daniel would call, and she didn't want her mama answering the phone.

John had convinced Mama to allow him to sleep in and skip church so that he could get to the ballpark by noon for warm-ups. Scanning the church sanctuary, Laura saw that there were quite a few faces missing from the regular congregation. Maybe because their church did not have an early morning service like Sydney's church, folks probably just skipped and went straight to the park for the softball finals. Daniel had not called last night. As the choir sung, she wondered what time his game was today and if he got to skip church.

The sun was blazing when Laura and Danielle stepped outside of the church. Deacon Harris came out right behind them and went to start up the church bus. Laura didn't see her grandma and knew there was no way Deacon Harris was leaving without her, so she took Danielle's hand and walked back toward the church and peeped inside the entryway. Grandma Annie was standing talking to a lady. So, she and Danielle stood inside the church entry for a few minutes reprieve from the heat.

"OK, girls, I'll see you all after the softball game," Grandma Annie shouted to Laura and Danielle as the church bus came to a stop in front of their house.

It was almost 1:30 p.m., and Aunt Nicky's maroon Ford Escort was parked in their driveway. Old-school music was blaring from the cassette player as they entered the living room. The girls kept walking toward the noise in the kitchen.

"Hey, girls, don't you all look pretty," Aunt Nicky greeted them as they walked into the kitchen.

Aunt Nicky was sitting at the kitchen table while Mama was finishing up frying the chicken. She joked about how Grandma Annie used to dress them up for church when they were little girls.

Her mama and Aunt Nicky were dressed casual in jean shorts, tank tops, and sandals. Not exactly what you would call church clothes.

"OK, girls, go change quickly so we can get down to the ballpark by 2:00 p.m.," Mama instructed them.

"Mama, I'm not going to go down to the ballpark." Laura pensively continued, "I'm going over and helping Grandma get the food ready for the victory dinner."

Laughing, her mama responded, "Laura, you know your grandma cooked most of that food last night, but OK, you can go over there instead of to the ballpark."

"Danielle!" Mama shouted down the hallway. "Are you ready?"

Danielle had copied their mama and Aunt Nicky's outfits. She came out the bedroom wearing a pair of jean shorts, t-shirt, and sandals. Even though Laura thought Danielle should wear sneakers, she didn't open her mouth. Laura didn't want her mama changing her mind about her not having to go to the ballpark.

The three of them backed out of the driveway with the car radio blaring out old-school music. Laura turned down the cassette player and sat on the couch. It wasn't too often that she got the house all to herself. The music with just the steady hum of the window air conditioner sounded and felt good. She leaned her head back on the couch and got lost in her thoughts about starting high school, the money she had saved for school clothes shopping, their final week on the tobacco farm, convincing Mama to buy a clothes dryer, and of course, Daniel. Let me just sit here for a few more minutes, she thought, then I'll change clothes and take the pan of fried chicken over to Grandma's house.

Oh no! Laura jumped up from the couch. The wall clock above the television was showing almost 3:00 p.m. The cassette player had stopped, and she knew the softball game would be ending soon. Laura rushed to the bedroom and quickly changed clothes. Not wanting to drop the pan of fried chicken, Laura rang the doorbell instead of trying to open the screen door.

"Hey, baby, what are you doing standing there? You didn't go to your brother's softball game?" Grandma Annie greeted her.

Her grandma held the screen door open wide so Laura could get inside while carrying the pan of chicken. Laura told her all about Saturday at the ballpark and how she came over to help her get Sunday dinner ready.

Grandma Annie had a hearty laugh, then said, "Child, this food is all ready, I'm just waiting for you all to get here. I made some potato salad, mac and cheese, fresh string beans, and baked a ham last night."

"A ham!" Laura exclaimed.

"Yep, for our victory dinner because I know them boys are going to win that final makeup game today," Grandma Annie said with jubilance in her voice.

They laughed in joyful agreement. Laura started getting the dishes out of the cabinet and placing them on the table. She watched Grandma Annie move around the small kitchen. Being around her grandma was warm and calming, no matter what the weather was outside.

"So, you got one more week to work in tobacco. Do you have your school shopping list all together?" Grandma Annie asked as she took two pitchers out of the cabinet and placed them on the kitchen counter.

Laura was glad to have the opportunity to have her grandma all to herself and just talk. She excitedly told her about the strategic shopping plans she and Sydney had made using the Sunday sales paper. They each had made a shopping list with the stores annotated. Her grandma was glad to hear the teens had an actual plan on how they wanted to spend their tobacco money. Working in tobacco all summer was not easy, and she didn't want the girls to waste their money. Grandma Annie was also delighted to hear that they were planning to ask Nicky to get them winter coats from the Kress store. The employee discount will definitely save a few dollars. Even though Laura never complained to her, Grandma Annie knew the young teen was getting tired of wearing Nicky's old clothes. Especially with starting high school.

"Grandma Annie, Mr. Isaiah and the three women we work with on the tobacco farm have been bringing us all a treat every Friday. Sydney and I want to take something for them next week on Thursday because we know they're probably going to bring us a treat for our last Friday. We don't know what to take because they have brought us fresh watermelon, pound cake, brownies, even pasta salad made with vegetables from their gardens," Laura explained.

Her grandma listened intently as Laura listed all of the different Friday treats. Standing at the counter putting a few more neatly sliced lemons into the pitcher of fresh lemonade and then dropping a few more into the pitcher of sweet tea, her grandma said, "Well, I didn't hear cookies on that list you just rattled off. I can bake you up a batch of chocolate chips. You know, I don't usually bake cookies until around the holiday season, but I think you girls finishing up working your first job, and on a tobacco farm at that, is something special."

"I love you, Grandma," Laura said as she wrapped her arms around the short, stocky woman.

About that time Danielle came bursting through the front screen door shouting, "We won! We won! We won!"

The jubilance of the day filled the house as her mama, Aunt Nicky, Uncle Richard, and his two girls all came bounding into the house behind Danielle. John had gone home to take a quick shower and change clothes. Her mama told Grandma that John had invited Angie Brown to the victory dinner.

"Please don't tease them at dinner," she added.

Grandma looked at Laura, smiled and winked. The dinner atmosphere was light and fun. John was the center of attention and how bad they beat the opposing team was the main topic of conversation. Laura was glad to have all the attention focused on John and off of her for a change. Uncle Richard's two girls were a couple of years older than Danielle, and they were John's three cheerleaders throughout the game. With her cousins in the bleachers, Danielle never even bugged their mama about going to the play area.

Everybody was too full to even think about dessert. Angie offered to help with the dishes, but Grandma Annie insisted that she and John go take a seat in the living room or on the front porch. Considering that the living room, dining room, and kitchen all flowed together with no walls, Laura wasn't surprised when they headed outside with their glasses of sweet tea in hand. Uncle Richard announced that he needed to get home because they had been gone practically all day. Grandma Annie fixed four to-go paper plates for him, his wife, and the girls. She also put four slices of chocolate cake on another paper plate. Laura was eyeing the ham as Grandma Annie covered it with foil on the stove. She was definitely planning on taking a ham sandwich for lunch tomorrow.

"Laura, Sydney's here," Danielle announced, looking out the living room window watching Uncle Richard and her cousins leave. She also saw Sydney walking toward the porch.

Sydney was like a member of their family. Walking into the house and greeting everyone with a big smile, she fit right in with the group of jovial women.

"Do you want something to eat?" Grandma Annie asked as she instinctively picked up a plate to start fixing food for Sydney.

"Thank you but no, ma'am. We just finished eating dinner not too long ago. My brother, Jacob, is sound asleep, and I think a movie is watching my mom and dad on the couch," Sydney responded.

Everybody had a good laugh.

"I see y'all had company for dinner," Sydney said to Laura as they left the kitchen area and went into the living room. "John introduced me to her when I came up on the porch. I've seen her at the softball games."

"Yes, girl, she also goes to our church," Laura giggled. "She seems nice though."

About that time, John and Angie came back into the house to say their goodbyes. They were going to catch the afternoon movie. Grandma insisted they take some of the chocolate cake with them. She cut up a couple of slices and wrapped them in foil.

"They better walk fast or all that chocolate icing is going to melt," Laura said to Sydney as the three of them, including Danielle, watched John and Angie leave from the big living room window.

"Let's go outside on the front porch," Laura said, tugging Sydney's arm. She didn't want to get pulled into her grandma, mama, and aunt's conversation because she was pretty sure John and Angie were going to be the main topic. Danielle was right at their heels as they headed outside. Sydney and Laura talked about the weekend's activities. Grandma Annie came outside to give the teens two glasses of lemonade. It was really hot on the porch, so she also took Danielle back inside to watch a little television. Laura knew her lil sister would be keeping a watchful eye on them from the living room window.

"Girl, I think it was hotter down at that park today than it was yesterday. After the game, Eric asked why you didn't come? He said the two tobacco twins are always together," Sydney exclaimed.

Both girls burst into laughter because they knew Eric was just being funny and not mean.

Taking a sip from her lemonade, Sydney continued, "One more week and we are done working on that tobacco farm!"

"Oh," Laura interjected, "my grandma said she'll bake some chocolate chip cookies for us to take on Thursday."

"Cool, I'll ask my mom to bake some too, because you know those guys can probably eat up some cookies," Sydney stated.

Grandma Annie brought out two slices of chocolate cake. The girls laughed and talked for almost another hour while sipping lemonade and eating cake. It had been a full day of church, softball, and family. The sun was starting to set, so Sydney said her goodbyes and headed home.

Danielle was sound asleep on Grandma Annie's couch. Getting her woke enough to walk home was not going to be easy, so Aunt

Nicky offered to drive them home. As Mama was attempting to rouse Danielle, Grandma Annie was packing food for them to carry home. She sliced multiple pieces of the succulent ham and wrapped them in foil. Laura didn't know what spices her grandma used to baste the ham, but it was delicious.

"Grandma, can I have a couple of extra slices of ham to take for lunch tomorrow?" Laura asked.

"Of course, baby," Her grandma answered and winked as she sliced more ham.

They finally got Danielle and the food into the back of Aunt Nicky's car. Laura was glad her aunt didn't bring up anything about shopping at Kress or tease her about tobacco money on the brief ride around the block. It had been a long day, a very good day, but still a long day. Everybody was ready to get home and prepare for Monday, the start to a new workweek and Laura's last week on the tobacco farm.

It was nearly 8:00 p.m., but Laura didn't want to take her bath yet just in case Daniel called. Primarily because she didn't want her mama to answer the phone. Laura helped her drowsy lil sis change into her pajamas. Danielle grabbed Scooby-Doo and fell right back to sleep. Laura went back into the kitchen and started to put the food away. She decided to go ahead and pack her lunch. Preferring her sandwich bread slightly toasted, she popped two slices of bread into the toaster. Just as she was finishing putting her lunch into the insulated lunch bag, the phone rang.

"I got it, Mama," Laura called out as she quickly made her way to the little corner table in the living room. Her mama barely looked up, she was relaxing and engrossed in watching a movie on the television.

"Hello," Laura said pensively.

"Hello, can I speak to Laura?" the voice on the other end asked.

"It's me," she said while starting to walk down the hallway with the phone. Not wanting to wake her sister, she went into the bathroom.

"You don't remember my voice?" she asked because she definitely remembered the deep, melodious sound of his voice.

"Of course, I do," he answered with a laugh. "But you sounded a little different, so I wanted to make sure it was you. How was your weekend?" Daniel continued.

"It was good. I went to Jacob and Mike's softball game. My brother plays on the same team with them, and they won all three games! I hope your team won," she said while sitting on the closed toilet fidgeting with her hair.

"Oh yeah!" Daniel responded with excitement in his voice. "We won and I made a couple of runs into home plate!"

Laura listened to him talk while imagining how good he must look in his white baseball uniform against that deep tanned face. She could see his broad smile and dimples peeping out from under his softball cap. She wondered if there was an Angie or a Carolyn in the stands cheering him on at his games. Laura stood up and looked at her reflection in the bathroom mirror. Daniel had only seen her in dirty and wet, tobacco-smelling work clothes.

"What do you plan on doing during the two-week break before school starts?" Daniel asked.

Before Laura could respond, Daniel hollered out "Laura" then "OK, I'm coming."

"Who were you talking to?" she asked.

"My mom," he responded. "She asked who was I talking to because she wants me to come and do something."

"You mean Mrs. Cindy knows you called me," Laura said with a sound of slight panic in her voice.

"Well, she does now, but it's OK," Daniel reassured her. "Do you have something to write with? I'll give you my phone number."

"OK, hold on for a minute," Laura said as she quickly went and got another one of the index cards and a pen from off the bedroom dresser. She went back into the bathroom and closed the door.

Daniel gave her his phone number and said, "I'll see you tomorrow, good night."

Laura barely responded because her brain was racing. Oh boy, she thought as she exited the bathroom and walked back down the hallway. Laura did not want to be the subject of Monday morning teasing by Mrs. Mary, Mrs. Cindy, and Miss Elaine. It was good-natured teasing, but she definitely didn't want their attention focused on her. Nor did she want Daniel's parents or David Jr. keeping a watchful eye on them during lunch break. Even though all they did was laugh and talk, but it was just the idea of them knowing that he had enough interest to call her in the evenings at home. As Laura placed the phone back on the little table in the living room, she was starting to feel a little angst about Monday morning on the tobacco farm. Her mama briefly looked up from the movie she was watching.

Laura took out her money envelope and placed the index card with Daniel's phone number inside then safely tucked it away in her top chest of drawer. She laid in the bed staring at the ceiling. Sleep didn't come easily like it normally did because she had a little anxiety at the thought of Mrs. Cindy knowing that she and Daniel were talking on the phone. What if she called him and Mrs. Cindy or his dad answered the phone…what would she say? She had never called a boy's house before. Laura glanced at the clock, and it was almost 10:00 p.m. Too late to call Sydney. Laura finally drifted off to sleep with all kinds of thoughts twirling in her head.

FINAL HARVEST WEEK

It was the start of their sixth and final week working on the tobacco farm! It had been a long, hot five weeks but here they were, still a full crew starting week six. Except for Laura, the morning porch chatter was in full swing as the young teens waited for Mr. Isaiah. Sydney noticed that her best friend was unusually quiet and not joining in on the morning bantering like she normally did.

"Hey, girl, you all right?" she asked Laura.

"You're not going to believe what happened last night," Laura whispered to Sydney just as Mr. Isaiah and Mr. Nate pulled up.

"Good morning, young folks!" Mr. Isaiah bellowed.

They had gotten so accustomed to his voice that it no longer sounded too loud. The young crew was also used to Mr. Wilson standing morning guard to see them off to the country and Mrs. Wilson standing afternoon guard to welcome them back home.

Mr. Wilson shouted to Mr. Isaiah and Mr. Nate, "I see the whole crew made it through the summer."

"Yes, they did; they are a good group of youngins!" Mr. Isaiah shouted back.

"Yep, they are!" Mr. Nate shouted also.

No one said anything, but from looking around the cargo bed of the truck at their faces Laura could tell everyone was pretty happy to get those positive accolades. Even Mr. Nate had spoken up! As they drove out of the neighborhood, Laura scooted over closer to Sydney.

In a very low voice, she leaned in and said, "Daniel called me last night. While we were talking, Mrs. Cindy called for him, and he told her that he was talking to me."

Sydney's eyes widened, and she whispered back, "Girl, no!"

Laura nodded her head up and down. She continued, "I hope Mrs. Cindy don't say anything about it this morning; you know how they like to tease."

The ride sure seemed awfully quick, Laura thought and sighed as Mr. Isaiah made the left turn down the rocky dirt road.

"Morning, Mary, final harvest week and the full crew is here!" Mr. Isaiah greeted her with a heightened level of excitement in his voice.

"Yes, they are, and these city girls have learned to string and loop like they were raised on a tobacco farm," she responded with motherly pride in her voice. "Come on, girls, let's get this week started."

The girls waved at Jacob and Mike as the truck headed up the road to the waiting damp field of tobacco. The three women were full of talk about their weekend. Anthony and Daniel had also won their softball games, but Laura already knew that. The two families had a joint celebration cookout at Mrs. Cindy's house on Sunday evening to celebrate. That's probably what Daniel had to help clean up, Laura thought. The three teens were quiet and just listened to the women talk. Mondays always required a little more concentration as they got their stringing and looping rhythm going for the week. Laura was silently praying that Mrs. Cindy wouldn't say anything about her and Daniel talking on the phone. The three women's conversation turned toward their couple of weeks break before starting back to work at Herd Elementary School. Laura was happy for the change in conversation.

The morning was humming right along. They were finishing up the third truck when they heard the familiar sound of the truck engines coming in for lunch. The morning had really sped by, and everybody was ready for a break. Laura had brought a nice, thick ham sandwich for lunch and was looking forward to eating it. During the whole six weeks, she had only eaten two slices of toast for breakfast each morning. By lunchtime, she was always hungry. All the guys jumped out of the back of the truck and headed toward the barn to gather the chairs and lunch coolers. Daniel stopped and greeted Laura first, as had become their routine.

The lunch conversation was extremely jovial. All the guys were hyped about winning their final softball games. David Jr. was also pretty excited about starting football practice next week. Laura was listening to the conversation, but she was also preoccupied watching Mrs. Cindy and Mr. David Sr. under the adult lunch tree. She wondered if they were chatting about her and Daniel.

She was so preoccupied that she almost missed Daniel saying to her, “Maybe we can go to one of the football games together since our schools play each other.”

Laura smiled at him as her anxiousness lifted. Watching a football game together sounded good. Maybe they could go to one of their homecoming games together. Daydreaming, she completely forgot about the transportation issue.

The afternoon shift sped by just as fast as the morning and not one of the women said anything about Laura and Daniel’s seemingly blooming friendship. Laura breathed a big sigh of relief once they were loaded back in the truck and headed home toward Ervinsville.

When the truck pulled up in front of Sydney’s house, everybody jumped out with a few grunts. Mondays always took a toll on their young bodies with the readjustment to the loading, standing, and constantly outstretched arms.

Amy and Mike walked up the street toward their homes, and Jacob went inside. Laura and Sydney stood there for a few minutes waiting for Sydney’s mom to go back inside.

“Girl, maybe Mrs. Cindy isn’t going to say anything,” Sydney said, moving in closer to Laura.

“Maybe not,” Laura told Sydney. “But Amy commented that I sure looked happy waving bye to Daniel after our lunch break.”

"Girl, you were grinning pretty hard," Sydney responded, and with that comment both girls went in to a fit of laughter.

"Well, you girls sure are happy for finishing up a long Monday on the tobacco farm," Mrs. Wilson said, observing the girls from the porch. She was still waiting for Sydney to come inside. Both girls giggled again, and Sydney went up the steps.

Danielle must have been watching for Laura from the living room window because she came bouncing out of the door full of energy as soon as she saw her sister approaching the house. Must be from all that sleep she got from going to bed so early last night, Laura thought while walking up the steps. It had been another sweltering hot August day. Grandma Annie came outside in one of her big flowery muumuu dresses and took a seat in one of the porch rocking chairs. Laura sat on the top step and asked her grandma for the shopping list for the cookies. She was planning to have John pick up the stuff from the grocery store tomorrow.

"I already got everything except the chocolate chips. Have him pick up a couple of bags and a box of those sandwich baggies to put the cookies in," Grandma Annie instructed Laura. Then she continued, "I plan to bake them on Wednesday evening after the sun goes down, so they'll be nice and fresh for your friends on Thursday."

"Laura, is Grandma baking cookies for your friend Daniel on the tobacco farm?" Danielle blurted out.

Laura quickly interjected, "No, the cookies are for all the people I work with on the tobacco farm."

Boy, that little girl has a memory like an elephant, Laura thought while giving her a quick side-eye. Grandma Annie didn't say a word, but Laura could tell by her raised left eyebrow that she definitely heard Danielle's question.

"Come on, Danielle, let's go home. Bye, Grandma, see you tomorrow," Laura said as she took her lil sister's hand to move her along a little faster off the porch.

Laura decided to watch some television and wait on the couch for John to come home. She tried her best to stay awake but must have dozed off because the sound of him coming in the front door startled her awake. The clock on the wall above the television read almost 10:00 p.m.; Monday was always a big restock day. John was surprised that Laura was still up as he greeted her and took a seat on the couch and started flipping through the channels. With a drowsy yawn, she started explaining to him about Grandma Annie baking the cookies and needing two bags of chocolate chips and a box of plastic sandwich baggies. He agreed to get the items and drop them off at their grandma's house. Laura gave her brother a couple of dollars and got up to go to bed. It would be 6:00 a.m. before her head barely touched the pillow. John went into the kitchen and took the foil-wrapped ham out of the refrigerator.

Tuesday and Wednesday went by fast. Jacob was leaning back with his eyes closed, soaking in the breeze as the big black truck made its way up the highway toward Ervinsville on Wednesday afternoon. Mike moved to the girls' side of the truck and was huddled in conversation with Amy.

Then he peered around Amy and said to Laura, "We only have two more days left on the tobacco farm. I bet you're going to miss your new friend."

Laura was aghast and pretended not to hear him over the breeze blowing into the back of the truck. Side-eyeing them, she saw Amy slightly elbow Mike.

"Ouch, I was just joking," he said.

Jacob never sat up or said a word, but Laura was pretty sure he wasn't that asleep. They both played sports with her brother, and she didn't want them blowing her friendship with Daniel all out of proportion. Mr. Isaiah pulled up in front of Sydney's house. Mike and Amy didn't waste any time leaving for home.

Laura and Sydney stayed on the sidewalk to talk.

"Obviously, Amy and Mike have been noticing me and Daniel sitting together at lunch," Laura commented.

"Girl," Sydney said. "Who hasn't noticed? Y'all been sitting together and talking every day for the last three weeks. Ever since Mr. David Sr. brought those extra folding chairs!"

Both girls laughed because Laura knew Sydney was telling the truth. They stepped closer together to talk because Sydney's mom was still sitting on the porch. After a few minutes of chatting, Sydney looked up and saw that her mom had gone inside.

"I'd better get in here and shower, just in case my mom needs some help finishing up the sugar cookies," Sydney said as she headed up the steps.

"I sure hope they like the cookies tomorrow," Laura said with excitement in her voice.

She lifted the oversized t-shirt over her head and started walking toward Grandma Annie's house. She really didn't care who saw her in the dirty work jeans because she felt good about having completed her very first paid job, even if it was working on a tobacco farm.

Laura hollered through the screen door, but there were no signs of Danielle or her grandma. She hollered again much louder. About that time her grandma was at the front screen door wearing her big apron with the lemons and limes all over it. Danielle was right beside her with a big oversized shirt on covered in flour.

"Child, we hear you, me and my little helper in here making cookies," Grandma Annie announced.

Laura looked at her lil sis and laughed. Aunt Nicky's old clothes sure had multiple uses.

"Grandma, can you put two cookies in each sandwich bag because Mrs. Wilson is making sugar cookies, and she's going to put two in each plastic baggie," Laura explained.

"Child, don't you worry; I'll have this all pretty and ready for you tomorrow morning. You'll be able to impress Daniel and friends," her grandma said, peering over the top of her glasses.

Danielle laughed. Laura was catching it from all circles today. She wondered if Daniel was being teased too.

"I told your brother to stop by on his way home from work and pick up the cookies. They'll be in your kitchen waiting for you when you get up in the morning," her grandma assured Laura.

"Oh, Grandma! You're the best," Laura praised her with a big smile.

Danielle stated with amusing firmness that she was spending the night with her grandma to help bake the cookies. Laura smiled inside knowing that she would have the house to herself for a few hours and her bedroom all night. That rarely happened; she was ready to go home. Grandma Annie and her lil helper went back inside the house to the kitchen, and Laura started home with just a little more pep in her step.

Ah, that felt good, Laura stretched as she put on her pajamas. She had taken a long leisurely bath instead of her usual shower. Her dish of Hamburger Helper noodles was smelling good coming from the oven. She had put it in the oven on the lowest setting to warm while she took her bath. Laura carried her bowl of food into the living room and settled on the couch to watch a little television. She found herself watching a couple of episodes of *Scooby-Doo*. Danielle's favorite show must be rubbing off on her, Laura laughed as she got up to take the empty bowl into the kitchen.

Laura poured herself a glass of half lemonade and half cherry Kool-Aid combination and decided to watch one more show. She was also kinda waiting for John to get home with the cookies. Just as she settled back onto the couch, the phone rang. Must be Sydney, she surmised while reaching for the phone.

"Hi, Laura, you're the only one that answers your phone," the deep voice teased her.

"Yes, I guess I'm the house telephone operator," she teased back.

They both had a good laugh and then chatted for a few minutes about the tobacco work coming to an end in a couple of days and school starting in just two weeks.

"My mom's talking about a trip down to Myrtle Beach, South Carolina, before school starts," Daniel informed her. "Maybe Labor Day weekend. It's not that far, just a couple of hours' drive. We'll probably drive down early Saturday morning, spend the night, and come back on Sunday because I know my dad is not going to drive in that Monday holiday traffic," he laughed.

"That sounds like fun," Laura responded, playing with her ear with one hand. Her family had only been to Robeson Lake with Aunt Nicky and Uncle Richard's family. She had never been to Myrtle Beach. She wondered if Daniel could swim and thought that he probably looked great in a pair of swim trunks.

"You know it's OK if you call me some time," Daniel said.

"OK, but I know you have stuff to do in the afternoons after we finish up work," Laura said, pushing back her hair.

"Yeah, but softball practice is over and things usually start to settle down around this time. I like ending my day talking to you," Daniel responded. "I'll see you tomorrow, good night."

Laura could feel her heart racing. She placed the phone back on the hook and glanced at the clock. It was almost 9:00 p.m. Laura sat there for a few minutes. She was still thinking about her conversation with Daniel while mindlessly watching a comedy on the television. When the show ended, she got up and went into the kitchen.

Everyone was gone, so Laura decided to measure the empty space beside the washer. She took out a tape measure, measured the space, and wrote the measurements down on an index card. Laura took the card to her bedroom and placed it in the envelope with her money and the other index card with Daniel's phone number. She stood there for a moment and picked up the card with Daniel's phone number. Looking at it, she thought, no way am I ready to call his house. Suppose Mrs. Cindy or Mr. David Sr. answered the phone. She was pretty sure David Jr. would just give the phone to

Daniel without asking her any questions. The two brothers seemed like they were really close. She reflected on watching them interact over the summer. Laura put the card back safely away in the envelope and closed the drawer. She laid down on her bed to wait for John to come home with the cookies.

It was almost 10:00 p.m. when John came in and placed the basket of chocolate chip cookies in the center of the kitchen table, taking a couple of bags for himself. That long, hot bath must have really relaxed Laura because she never even heard her brother come home. The sound of the blaring 6:00 a.m. alarm clock woke her up. Hitting the alarm clock, she glanced over at Danielle's bed, remembering that her lil sis had spent the night with Grandma. It felt a little odd. Laura could not even remember the last time she and Danielle had spent the night apart. She was excited and anxious to see how Grandma Annie had prepared the cookies, so Laura made a beeline for the kitchen. Sitting in the center of the table was a large basket with a handle and a flip top cover. Laura lifted the cover and exclaimed, "Oh my goodness!"

Her grandma had filled the basket to the brim with sandwich baggies of chocolate chip cookies. Grandma Annie was a gem, Laura smiled as she walked back down the hallway toward the bathroom.

Before leaving the house, Laura took a few packages of the chocolate chip cookies and put them on a plate. She left the plate on the kitchen counter beside the coffee pot.

Walking up to the porch, Laura saw a round straw basket with a handle sitting on the little table on Sydney's porch. Greeting everyone, Laura noticed that Amy seemed a little annoyed.

Sydney spoke up. "I told Amy that we didn't intentionally leave her out of bringing cookies for the crew today."

Oh, so that's what's wrong with her this morning, Laura mused. Laura slightly touched Amy's arm and said, "Girl, don't worry about that, my grandma baked enough cookies for five crews. Any more cookies and we'd all be too full on a sugar high to finish the afternoon shift."

Everybody laughed, including Amy, and the damper mood lifted right as Mr. Isaiah pulled up. Today was Thursday, one more morning pickup. Laura and Sydney placed the two baskets in front of them and held on to the top of the handles. Both girls made sure the basket lids were secure. They didn't want cookies spilling out all over the cargo bed of the truck.

Mrs. Mary noticed right away that the girls were carrying two baskets in addition to their regular lunch containers. The girls tried to place the baskets in the darkest, coolest spot on the back table before taking their positions to begin stringing tobacco. Mrs. Cindy and Miss Elaine also looked curiously at the baskets.

"You girls sure brought a lot of extra food today," Mrs. Mary commented.

All three girls had big smiles on their faces. Laura was happy that Amy's mood had lifted because they all had gotten along really good all summer, and she had just genuinely forgotten to talk to Amy about the cookie surprise. She was used to planning and doing things with Sydney.

During the morning stringing and looping sessions, Mrs. Mary and the other women were discussing that even though they were finishing up harvesting the last field of tobacco, more work still had to be done by the menfolk to finish up the season. They won't rotate anymore looped tobacco out to the second barn. The final tobacco in each barn will be taken and sold within the next week. Then they had to get the fields ready for replanting. Laura and the girls listened to the women as they rhythmically talked and strung the tobacco. Tobacco farming was definitely a continual process with some very long days.

Finally lunchtime came, and the women were super curious to find out what the three girls had in those baskets. Mr. Isaiah and Mr. Nate, always moving quickly with precision timing, dropped the guys off and were on their way back up the road. Laura and Sydney wanted to give them some cookies for the rest of the crew, but that would have to wait until they came back to pick up the guys.

"Hey," Daniel grinned, walking up to Laura, "I heard y'all brought us some cookies." He greeted her with a big smile.

She knew those guys couldn't keep anything. Jacob and Mike probably told the guys as soon as they got out to the tobacco field.

"Hi," Laura smiled back. "My grandma baked some chocolate chip cookies, and Sydney's mom baked some sugar cookies."

"Well, I want some chocolate chips," he announced as they walked toward the barn.

"Me too." David Jr., said, walking up right behind them.

Laura jumped and almost tripped because she didn't realize that David Jr. was walking that closely behind them. Daniel reached out and grabbed her arm to steady her from falling. The two teens stood close to each other all the time but had never really touched, except for that one time when Laura had given Daniel her phone number on the index card. His hand felt firm but gentle as he held her arm while she steadied herself.

"There's no need to wait to pass out the cookies because all the guys already know about them," Laura said to Sydney as they reached the teen lunch tree.

"I know, our lunch break goes by so fast, let's go ahead and pass them out to the adults first," Sydney recommended.

Laura motioned to Amy and the three girls walked over to the adult lunch tree carrying the two baskets.

Approaching the adult tree, Laura began. "Ah, excuse us, but we just wanted to thank y'all for being so kind and patient teaching us the tobacco ropes and always bringing us treats on Friday."

"We brought some homemade cookies for everybody!" Sydney chimed in with a big smile.

Laura and Sydney unclasped and lifted the lids on the two baskets. With the heat, the smell of chocolate chips and buttery sugar permeated the air. Amy passed out a bag of chocolate chip and a bag of sugar cookies to each adult. The women were beaming and bragging to the menfolk about how good of workers the girls were and how quickly they picked up cropping the tobacco. Mrs. Mary took a bite of one of the sugar cookies and declared how sweet and nice it was. The rest of the adults didn't require much nudging to start eating their cookies too. Mrs. Cindy took a bite of one of the chocolate chips.

"Did you girls bake these homemade cookies yourself?" Mrs. Mary asked.

"No, ma'am," Sydney spoke up. "My mom baked the sugar cookies, and Laura's grandma baked the chocolate chips."

"Well, please tell them thank you because these are some mighty fine cookies!" Mr. Roy said, eating both chocolate chip and sugar cookies.

Everybody laughed.

"Hey! Can we get some of those cookies over here?" Anthony hollered over to them.

There was even more laughter as the girls went over to the teen lunch tree and handed out cookies. There was so much cheerfulness and joking around the lunch trees that you would have thought it was a Friday.

They started picking up the chairs and lunch coolers, signaling the end of the lunch break, when Mr. David Sr. asked, "Hey, young ladies, how about giving us a few bags of those cookies for an afternoon snack?"

"Yes, sir, y'all can take the whole basket. We brought enough to share with Mr. Isaiah and the rest of the field crew," Laura responded.

"No, he cannot," Mrs. Cindy said and laughed. "He'll eat the whole basket."

Mr. David Sr. did a playful pout.

Laura thought their playful bantering was cute. She had rarely seen adult couples interacting playfully with each other. She suspected that was where Daniel got his teasing nature.

Sydney spoke up with a recommendation to put some of each kind in both baskets and give one of the baskets to Mr. Isaiah for the crew and then keep the second basket at the barn until the end of the day for everybody to carry some home.

"That's a good plan," Mrs. Cindy said. "Cause my Daniel loves chocolate chip cookies."

Both Mrs. Cindy and Mr. David Sr. burst into laughter again. Oh my gosh, they know was all Laura could think. Daniel just shook his head and continued walking toward the barn with the chairs without looking back at his parents.

As the crew got back into stringing position and started working on the afternoon truckload of tobacco, Laura peered around the table. These women talked about everything, so Mrs. Cindy had to have told Mrs. Mary and Miss Elaine that Daniel was calling her in the evenings after work. She was glad they had decided not to publicly tease her.

Laura was melancholy and happy at the same time about tomorrow being Friday, their last day on the tobacco farm. The final truck of the day was really loaded down with tobacco. Mrs. Mary, Mrs. Cindy, and Miss Elaine were moving their hands at lightning speed to get it finished by the time the guys came in from the field. Laura and the girls sped up as well but not nearly as fast as the women.

"Whew!" Mrs. Mary said as the three trucks turned one behind the other down the dirt road. "We finished just in time." Putting her hands on her hips, she continued, "Y'all know them trucks going to be loaded down tomorrow to finish up this tobacco harvest."

Mrs. Cindy and Miss Elaine were nodding their heads in agreement. Laura, Sydney, and Amy gave each other knowing looks, acknowledging that their last Friday was going to be a super busy tobacco stringing and looping day. Mr. Isaiah jumped out of the truck and walked with the cookie basket toward the three girls. He was such a tall giant of a man that the cookie basket looked extra tiny as the handle dangled from his big hands.

"Thank you so much for those delicious homemade cookies," he said with a big grin while handing the basket back to Sydney.

Meanwhile, Mrs. Mary, always the leader, took the second basket of cookies and put several bags in her, Mrs. Cindy's, and Miss Elaine's coolers. She also left a few bags of cookies in the basket for the young teen crew.

Mr. Kevin saw them dividing up the cookies and said, "Hey, I'm a single man, don't I get some cookies to take home?"

"No," Mrs. Mary responded with a twinkle in her eyes. "You just take a little ice cream over to Elaine's this evening, and I'm sure she'll share her cookies with you."

Everybody standing near the back table had a good end-of-day laugh. Miss Elaine just shook her head at them because she was so used to their relationship teasing.

Daniel was standing by Laura as she picked up her insulated lunch bag off the table. "Those were some really good cookies, especially the chocolate chips," he said to Laura while reaching into his overall pocket and pulling out a plastic baggie with two chocolate chip cookies. "I saved a couple for the ride home," he said with a wink. "Tell your grandma I said thanks. I'll see you tomorrow."

He ran toward his family truck and jumped in the back. Laura was beaming as she climbed into the back of Mr. Isaiah's truck. She had never had a boy show this much attention toward her. Laura kinda glided through junior high in Aunt Nicky's ill-fitting hand-me-downs relatively unnoticed. Come to think of it, all Daniel had ever seen her in was loose, ill-fitting jeans and oversized men's t-shirts. Go figure that, she laughed.

"Earth to Laura, earth to Laura," Sydney said as the truck headed up the dirt road.

"Girl, stop," Laura responded with a laugh.

Tomorrow, Friday, their last day on the tobacco farm, was going to be bittersweet, she reasoned as the truck turned onto the two-lane paved road toward Ervinsville. Perched on the porch, Mrs. Wilson patiently waited for the safe return of the young crew. They had all gotten used to her welcoming end-of-day smile. Laura was already used to Mrs. Wilson's kind demeanor prior to working in tobacco, but truthfully it still felt good to have her welcome them back home every evening.

"Hi, Isaiah, these young folks made it six whole weeks!" she greeted him with a big proud mama smile.

"Yes, they did," he bellowed back. "Thanks so much for the homemade cookies, the crew loved them."

"It was my pleasure," she responded. "You know it was all the girls' idea. Sydney talks all the time about how nice the ladies are that you have them working with."

"Yep, they're all really good people; I've known them most of my life," he bellowed back with warmth in his voice. "I'll see you young folks bright and early tomorrow morning; it's a big day." With that statement he was gone.

"Here, Amy, you and Mike can take these few bags of cookies that are left," Laura offered. "I just want to take one bag of sugar cookies for Danielle," she added while handing the basket to Amy.

"And I will take one more bag of those chocolate chips," Jacob said as he grabbed a bag and ran up the porch steps.

"I'll also just take one bag of those chocolate chips," Sydney said while taking a bag out of the basket.

Everybody laughed while Amy put the few remaining bags in her and Mike's lunch containers. It was a sweet ending to what turned out to be a really fun working Thursday.

Laura walked with an extra pep in her step toward her grandma's house as she thought about her final payday. She had started out wanting to buy clothes, clothes, and more clothes. Oh, she definitely still wanted lots of new school clothes, but she also wanted to do a couple of other things. She had pretty much saved almost all of her pay since the first week. It would be at least ten months before another summer job came around.

Laura was so deep in thought that she didn't hear Eric calling her name.

"Hey, Laura," he called louder and for the third time.

She looked in the direction of his voice. Eric was approaching the intersection where she crossed over to keep straight to her grandma's. She instinctively pulled the dirty t-shirt over her head before he caught up with her.

"Hi, Laura, how you doing? I haven't seen you and your buddy up to the schoolyard this week," Eric said all in one breath.

"Yeah, it's been a busy week with work and all," Laura responded while fidgeting with the empty cookie basket. That August sun was hot, and she just wanted to get Danielle and go home.

"Oh, when do you finish up on the tobacco farm because school starts in a couple of weeks?" Eric asked.

"Tomorrow's our last day," she announced with a big smile.

"Oh cool, I know you and Sydney will be happy," Eric stated.

"Yep, we sure will. I'll see you later." Laura ended the conversation and started to walk away.

Eric turned to go in the opposite direction toward Sydney's house. Laura hadn't seen her lil sis in twenty-four hours and was actually looking forward to seeing the little squirt. Danielle came bouncing out the front door full of energy.

"Hey, Laura, did everybody like the cookies?" she asked with excitement in her voice.

"Yep, they loved them and ate them all up except for this one bag of sugar cookies that I saved just for you," Laura said, handing the plastic sandwich bag to Danielle. "They're a little broken but still good."

"Yay!" Danielle wailed as she took the bag from Laura's hand.

"What's all this commotion?" Grandma Annie said, stepping out onto the porch.

Danielle held up the plastic sandwich bag of sugar cookies. Laura told her grandma all about the day's happenings and how everybody really enjoyed the cookies. She even told her grandma that her chocolate chip cookies were a big hit. The whole crew sent many thanks to her and Mrs. Wilson.

"I'm glad to hear Daniel and all your friends from the tobacco farm enjoyed the cookies," her grandma stated with teasing in her voice.

Danielle laughed and Laura exclaimed, "Grandma, we're all just friends, and besides tomorrow is my last day."

Danielle went inside to get her stuff from the overnight stay.

"So, tomorrow's your last day." Grandma Annie continued, "I know you've made some new friends on the tobacco farm, but you'll also meet some new friends in high school in a couple of weeks. Some of your old friends from junior high will be there also."

Laura knew it was her grandma's way of preparing her for the possibility of never seeing her tobacco farm friends again after tomorrow. When something happened, whether it was good or bad, Laura had often heard her grandma say, "Life changes just like the seasons of the year."

Like a burst of energetic wind, Danielle came out the front door with her Scooby-Doo backpack. Laura was surprised that screen was still intact, the way her lil sis ran in and out that door all summer. Danielle zipped down the steps with a quick bye Grandma. Grandma Annie gave the lil girl a funny pouty face, and she darted back up the steps and gave her grandma a quick hug. That sugar from all the chocolate chip taste testing the night before was working!

Laura watched her lil sis walking slightly ahead and swinging her Scooby-Doo backpack. Danielle would be starting fourth grade, and their mama always seemed to manage to get the lil girl a few new outfits for school. Probably because children's clothes were not as expensive as teen clothes. Laura had seen that when she took Danielle to Kress store to get her a couple of summer outfits. Maybe I'll get her a new Scooby-Doo backpack, Laura contemplated as they reached the intersection. Danielle took off running, with her pigtails and backpack flying in the air toward the little gray cement porch. Yeah, she full of sugar, Laura laughed.

Even after her bath Danielle was still hyped, so Laura agreed to let her watch one more thirty-minute show. While they were sitting on the couch watching television, the phone rang.

"Hey, girl, tomorrow's Friday and our last payday," Sydney's voice greeted her.

"I know, I can't wait for next week so we can actually do some clothes shopping," Laura responded while getting up and walking into the hallway toward the bedroom with the phone.

"My mom's having me keep back one complete paycheck for school activities," Sydney continued. "You know, for stuff like going to the games or even the county fair that's coming in September."

"Girl, that's not a bad idea," Laura responded out loud while thinking to herself that she would separate out her money on Friday evening after work.

The conversation changed from clothes to boys. "Do you really think you'll see Daniel anymore after tomorrow?" Sydney asked.

Leaning back on her pillow, Laura joked pensively, "I don't know, you know the bus don't make no runs outside the city limits. David Jr. can drive, but he don't have a car. Anyways, I just want to get through tomorrow."

"Me too," Sydney agreed, and they ended their call as Danielle came into the bedroom.

Glancing at the clock, it was just after 9:00 p.m. and her lil sis had finally fallen off to sleep. Laura eased out of the bed, not wanting to wake Danielle back up, and went into the kitchen to get a drink of water. Laura sat at the kitchen table thinking about tomorrow when the phone rang again. She thought, what did Sydney forget to tell me? Walking into the living room, she picked up the phone and said, "Hey, girl."

The deep voice came back. "Hey, but I'm not a girl."

They both laughed as she sat down on the couch and said, "I thought you was Sydney."

"Nope," he responded with teasing in his voice.

They continued talking for a few minutes. Talking to Daniel on the phone was not as awkward as Laura had thought it would be. She always visualized his face and the conversation flowed smoothly.

She heard the key in the front door as Daniel was saying something about him and Anthony catching rides into town next weekend and maybe meeting up at the mall food court.

Laura quickly responded, "That sounds great, let's talk about it tomorrow."

She hung up the phone and sat there for a few minutes thinking that a meetup at the mall food court sounded great.

John greeted her as he walked into the house but kept walking toward the kitchen. Coming back into the living room with a glass of juice and bag of cookies, he noticed the silly grin on Laura's face and asked, "What are you grinning at?"

"Tomorrow is my last day working on the tobacco farm!" Laura responded with enthusiasm. Even though she was actually thinking about Daniel and a possible meetup at the mall.

"John, do you give Mama money year-round to help with the bills?" Laura asked as he turned on the television.

She had been curious about it for a while but especially now since she hadn't given up on the idea of convincing their mama to get a clothes dryer. Once school started John would primarily work part-time on the weekends and maybe one or two days through the week. His schedule was too busy with sports during the school year to put in much time at the grocery store.

"Yeah, maybe five or ten dollars depending on how much I make. Why, are you looking to get a part-time job now that your tobacco job is ending?" John asked her.

"No, but I'm still trying to convince Mama to get a clothes dryer for the winter months," Laura explained.

"That would be nice. Because I have brought in plenty of frozen jeans," he said, leaning back on the couch.

"Yep, me too," Laura said as she got up from the couch. "We'll see what happens, good night," she told her brother as she went into the kitchen to rinse out her glass before going to bed.

Laura had a restless night of sleep. Her mind kept racing with thoughts of how different this Friday would be from the other five Fridays. The guys had said the fields were pretty much bare, and there was just a little tobacco left to harvest. Knowing Mr. Isaiah and Mr. Nate, they probably had it calculated down to the last truck. They ran their tobacco farming operation with precision timing.

At some point, Laura must have finally dozed off to sleep because the blaring 6:00 a.m. alarm clock woke her up. Staring at her face in the mirror, Friday payday and our last workday, Laura thought while brushing her teeth.

Happy, excited, anxious, coupled with a bit of anxiety, Laura was a ball of emotions as she approached Sydney's house. Everybody was already gathered on the front steps talking about the day ahead and plans for the upcoming two weeks before school started.

"That time will go by so fast," Mike was saying as Laura walked up and greeted the group.

"Yeah, we were talking to the guys yesterday about meeting up at the mall or the school playground for a pickup softball game before school starts," Jacob added.

Laura remembered last night's conversation with Daniel when he had said that he and Anthony may come to the mall next weekend. Like clockwork, the big black shining truck turned the corner, and Mr. Isaiah pulled up at precisely 7:00 a.m.

"Good morning, young folks, let's get this harvest done!" he bellowed through the open window.

Mr. Nate gave them his customary nod. They all quickly loaded into the back of the truck as Mr. Wilson stepped out on to the porch. Laura watched him as he greeted Mr. Isaiah. He and Mrs. Wilson were definitely a tag team. Everybody was in a good mood about their last workday. Looking around the truck, Laura thought that maybe she was the only one with a little angst about it being their last day on the tobacco farm.

Trying to think about something else, she leaned over to Sydney and said, "I saw Eric when I was walking home yesterday. Did he stop by your house?"

"Yeah, he stopped by and talked to Jacob for a few minutes. Girl, I heard his voice on the porch, but I didn't come back outside. Jacob had already taken his shower, and I was ready for my turn in the bathroom," Sydney responded with hand motions.

Both girls laughed with a knowing understanding of the need for that afternoon shower.

"Next week, we'll be able to sleep in and have a few normal days before school starts back up," Sydney blissfully added.

Laura's kinda melancholy mood started to lift as they drove down the highway out of the city and toward the tobacco farm. She leaned back and soaked in the early morning breeze as they approached the turnoff point.

With a huge dose of extra cheerfulness in her voice, Mrs. Mary greeted the young crew. As the girls jumped out of the back of the truck, she proclaimed, "Let's get this harvest wrapped up!"

"Yes, indeed!" Mr. Isaiah shouted back as he turned the truck around and was off to the field to load up the last of the tobacco crop.

The teens put up their lunches and took their positions at the worktable. Mrs. Cindy passed out an index card to each of them.

Mrs. Cindy, Mrs. Mary, and Miss Elaine's names, addresses, and phone numbers were written on them.

Mrs. Mary explained, "We want y'all to keep in touch and let us know how your first year of high school is going. If you girls approach your schoolwork the same way you approached working out here this summer, y'all will be just fine."

Laura looked at her card and thought everybody must have a stack of these school index cards at home. The information was neatly handwritten. She recognized Mrs. Cindy's home phone number because Daniel had already given it to her. Laura had the number memorized even though she had never dialed it. The girls thanked the women profusely for the contact information and promised to keep in touch as they placed the cards safely in their jean pants pockets.

Grabbing leaves of tobacco for stringing, the girls voiced their excitement about starting high school. Usually, the girls worked relatively quietly as they tried to keep their stringing rhythm steady and just listened to the women talk about their lives and families To Laura's surprise, her hands did not slow down as the girls told the women about their plans for school shopping, high school activities, and classes. All three girls were planning to take first-year Spanish and most likely would be in the same class together. The atmosphere was happy and positive as they swiftly finished up the first truckload of tobacco.

The morning was moving right along; the girls were taking a quick break as Mr. Nate backed the third truckload of tobacco up to the overhang worktable. Only taking her usual half a cup of water, Laura looked around, surveying the area. The big lunch trees, as they were now called, looked so tranquil and welcoming. In a way they reminded her of the three women. Laura definitely planned to keep in touch, maybe she'd give them a call at Thanksgiving or during Christmas break. She had learned a lot just listening to them talk. They all seemed to be a very tight-knit community, even though they didn't live in a community like hers with multiple streets and houses grouped together. Laura still didn't quite understand all the dynamics of living in the country, but working on the tobacco farm all summer turned out to be much better than she had anticipated, even with the long, hot, tiring days. And she met Daniel, Laura smiled as she took her position to start the third truck.

It was lunchtime already, and they were just finishing up the last few tobacco leaves in the third truck. The whole crew had picked up their looping speed to get the truck finished by lunchtime. Laura looked at the fourth truck, as the guys came rolling in for lunch, and it was also loaded down with tobacco.

"Them young boys been pushing themselves hard today to get the last bit of this harvest done," Mr. Roy said as he jumped out of the passenger side of Mr. Isaiah's truck.

"Yes, they have; we should finish right on time this afternoon!" Mr. Isaiah echoed. "My wife sliced up some more watermelon last night. She knew today was going to be a hard push and thought y'all might enjoy something sweet and cold for lunch. I told her about them good cookies yesterday, and she wanted to know why I didn't bring her any," he said and laughed heartily while lifting a large cooler out of the back of his truck.

David Jr. took his family's cooler to the teen lunch tree instead of to the adult tree. The three women were standing under the teen tree. Laura also noticed that Mr. Isaiah and Mr. Nate had not left like they normally do at lunchtime; they were sitting under the adult tree with the other men.

Mrs. Mary announced, "To celebrate the end of harvest and these young people working with us all summer, we've got a special lunch prepared for everybody."

The three women passed out lunch plates with two pieces of freshly fried chicken, corn on the cob, tomato and cucumber salad with a vinaigrette, and a homemade biscuit. Laura knew the corn, tomatoes, and cucumbers were from their gardens. The food was so delicious, nobody was even talking, just eating and enjoying their special lunch. Mrs. Mary, always thinking of everything, had a big trash bag for them to put the paper plates in after eating. Mr. Isaiah allowed some extra time for lunch, so the ladies passed out some slices of the watermelon. Oh, that cold, sweet watermelon was the perfect dessert, Laura thought as she took a bite.

The lunch conversations were starting to pick back up as everyone ate the watermelon. It was pretty clear the guys had already talked about meeting up next Saturday. They had all become pretty good friends over the past six weeks. Amy chimed in on the guys' conversation and offered a suggestion that they all meet at the mall food court for lunch and then maybe go to the matinee together or to the ballpark.

"Oh yeah!" Anthony said. "The *Smokey and the Bandit II* movie is coming out next week. Man, did you see that Pontiac Firebird Trans-Am in the first movie? It was sweet."

Mrs. Mary interrupted their conversation to get them to put the watermelon rinds in the trash bag. It was time to finish up the harvest! Everybody was in a good mood and ready to finish the afternoon shift.

Daniel walked beside Laura back to the barn and said, "Next Saturday sounds like a plan. I saw the first *Smokey and the Bandit,* and it was pretty good. We'll probably be at the mall a few hours before noon because I want to get some new sneakers."

"Oh, OK, I'm going to do some school shopping next week myself," Laura was saying when David Jr. shouted out for Daniel to hurry up.

Laura and Daniel turned around, not realizing how slowly they were walking because all the guys were already in the back of the truck.

"OK, talk to you later," he said, lightly touching her arm and then taking off running toward the truck.

Laura was too engrossed in watching Daniel jog away to notice Mrs. Cindy watching her with a smile. Her Daniel seemed to have taken a real liking to Laura.

About 3:00 p.m., Mr. Nate came driving down the dirt road with the fifth load of the day. The truck looked like it was wobbling from side to side due to the amount of tobacco stuffed in the back. Mrs. Mary had said that sometimes they worked a little later on the last harvest day to finish up any remaining tobacco. While taking a quick break during the truck swap out, the girls commented that there was no way there was going to be anymore tobacco. Since this morning, every truck had been loaded down.

As Mr. Nate drove off, Laura was wondering what the guys were doing if this was the last truckload of tobacco.

Sydney must have read her mind because she spoke up and asked, "Do you think the guys are still harvesting more tobacco?"

"Well," Mrs. Mary began, "They could be finishing up the last couple of rows, they could have rode up to Walker's Corner Store, or they could be relaxing in the back of one of them trucks under a tree enjoying some more of that nice cold watermelon."

All of them burst into a fit of laughter but their hands kept right on stringing and looping at a rapid rhythmic pace. Laura had gotten so used to the sound and timing of the trucks that she knew the trucks were coming in a little early. They still hadn't finished the 3:00 p.m. truckload, and one of the incoming trucks was half full of tobacco! She pulled out her watch and glanced at the time. It was just about 4:45 p.m. All the guys quickly scurried out of the first truck when it came to a stop. Mr. Isaiah jumped out and addressed Mrs. Mary. He wanted to know if she, Mrs. Cindy, and Miss Elaine could stay a couple of extra hours and finish up the last bit of tobacco while he took the teens home. Mrs. Mary readily agreed because the women were already expecting to have to stay a little longer.

Mr. Isaiah handed out the three white envelopes to the teen girls for the last time. Laura folded hers in half, put it in her jeans pocket, and then patted her pocket for reassurance. Her final $200.

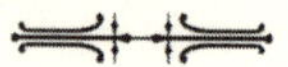

The teens were getting ready to load up into the truck when Mr. Roy announced that he and Mr. David Sr. had given Anthony, Daniel, and David Jr. permission to ride with Mr. Isaiah to take the town crew home. Mr. David Sr. added that the menfolk were going to wait at the barn and keep the ladies company while they finished up the last bit of tobacco. Laura and Sydney looked at each other—they didn't see that coming. Laura looked at Daniel. He was trying not to grin too much but couldn't help himself, those dimples on his cheeks were in full bloom.

The back of the truck was big and spacious with the side benches, but Laura was glad David Jr. got into the cab of the truck with Mr. Isaiah. Of course, Amy and Mike sat beside each other. Daniel took the seat on the opposite side of Mike and motioned for Laura to sit beside him. Sydney, Jacob, and Anthony sat on the opposite side. Laura noticed that there were four watermelons and four brown paper bags up against the back of truck. She assumed Mr. Isaiah was giving them watermelons but was curious as to what was in the bags. Everybody was leaning back, talking and enjoying the breeze. Daniel had scooted down closer to her on the bench, allowing space between him and Mike. His right leg was touching right up next to Laura's left leg as everyone talked about the end of work and having two-weeks free time before school started. Laura could hardly concentrate on the conversation because she had never had a boy sit this close to her. During lunch they always sat in the individual folding chairs.

"What's in those bags?" Laura asked out loud to no one in particular.

"Oh," Daniel said, touching her leg as to acknowledge that he was going to answer the question.

When she looked in his direction, he removed his hand and continued with, "We finished up early in the tobacco field, so we rode out to Mr. Isaiah's house with him while my dad and the other men took a break."

"Yeah," Anthony joined in on the explanation. "We knew that y'all hadn't finished the fourth truck because it was loaded down with tobacco."

Daniel continued, "Mr. Isaiah's wife had fixed up all these bags of fresh cucumbers, tomatoes, and peppers. So, she gave some bags to us along with the watermelons.

"Oh, that was really nice of her," Sydney said.

Jacob had not said too much during the ride home, as usual he was leaning back with his eyes closed as though he was asleep. Laura knew that even though he was a year younger than her brother, John, they still hung out together in the same circle of friends. She wondered if Jacob or Mike had mentioned Daniel to her brother.

As they were entering the city, Anthony asked, "Do y'all live in the same neighborhood?"

Jacob, all of a sudden, spoke up with, "Yeah, Mike, Amy, and us all live on the same street, and Laura lives two streets over."

So, as Laura had speculated, he really wasn't asleep. Just resting but definitely listening.

Mr. Isaiah turned the corner down their street but drove right past Jacob and Sydney's house. All of the city crew had questioning looks on their faces as Mr. Isaiah drove up the street and made a U-turn, then pulled up in front of Amy's house. He jumped out of the driver's side of the truck's cab and announced that he remembered where everyone lived from the last time he had given them watermelons. He decided to make it a complete circle back to his turnoff point.

He shook Amy's hand, thanked her for doing a great job, and gave her a watermelon and bag of vegetables. Sydney and Laura hollered out to Amy that they would call her to coordinate going shopping. He repeated the same thing at Mike's house. Then Mr. Isaiah went back down the street and stopped in front of Jacob and Sydney's house.

Instead of sitting on the porch waiting for them, Mrs. Wilson was standing on the bottom of the steps.

"Hey, Isaiah," she greeted him. "I saw you drive past the house and came down here to look and see where you was taking my youngins."

They both had a hearty laugh as he explained to her about his wife sending the watermelons and vegetables.

"Oh, fellas." He turned back to the truck and said, "This is Mrs. Wilson, Jacob and Sydney's mom. She baked those delicious sugar cookies."

David Jr., Daniel, and Anthony all shouted, "Thank you!"

"OK, fellas, one more stop down the other end of this street, then we'll be headed back home," Mr. Isaiah bellowed.

"Bye, I'll call you later," Sydney shouted and waved as the truck pulled away.

Laura waved back, but her mind was on the next stop.

"I thought Jacob said you lived two streets over," Daniel stated inquisitively.

The truck had emptied out, but he still had not moved from sitting close to Laura.

"Oh, my Grandma Annie lives here, I have to pick up my lil sister, Danielle," Laura managed to say as Mr. Isaiah pulled up in front of the house.

Daniel jumped out the back of the truck and took Laura's hand to help her jump out also. Laura giggled inside, knowing full well that she had been jumping in and out of the back of that truck for the past six weeks all by herself. Anthony handed the watermelon and bag of vegetables to Daniel. Mr. Isaiah also got out of the truck and closed the driver's side door. It sounded like a loud thud, so

Laura knew with all the commotion Grandma Annie was coming to the screen door.

And sure enough, her grandma stepped out on to the porch. "Hey, Laura, what's going on out here with all these handsome fellas!" she greeted them, peering over her glasses with a big smile.

Danielle came out right behind her. Grandma Annie was very charming, and all the guys were grinning from ear to ear, including Mr. Isaiah.

"Hi, Grandma, this is Mr. Isaiah and David Jr., Anthony, and Daniel," Laura introduced the group.

"Daniel! Daniel!" Danielle exclaimed.

His face lit up, and everybody broke out into laughter as Danielle came down the steps to get a closer look. Daniel shook the lil girl's hand and gave her a big smile.

"Laura has been a great worker, and I really appreciate her sticking with it all summer to help us get the harvest in," Mr. Isaiah told Grandma Annie. "And thank you so much for those delicious chocolate chip cookies."

"Yes, ma'am, they were very good!" Anthony and Daniel said simultaneously.

"They sure were, thank you, ma'am!" David Jr. said from the truck's cab.

Grandma Annie was beaming from all the compliments!

"Well, we need to be on our way," Mr. Isaiah said as he clasped Laura's hand and thanked her again for doing a good job on the tobacco farm. He also added that he hoped to see their crew again next year. Well, I don't know about that, Laura thought to herself as she smiled back at him. Even though, over the six weeks, she had really grown to admire Mr. Isaiah. Besides being the most punctual person ever, he was always very kind to the young teen crew. Mr. Isaiah walked back around the truck and jumped into the driver's side.

Daniel leaned in, touched Laura's arm, and said, "I'll call you this weekend." Then he jumped back into the cargo bed of the truck.

Laura and Danielle waved and stood there watching until the truck made the first right turn at the corner intersection. As the truck disappeared around the corner, Laura turned around to find Grandma Annie watching her from the porch.

Danielle declared, "I like Daniel—his name is almost like mines!"

"Well, I guess that settles that," Laura said with a laugh.

"Mr. Isaiah seem like a good man," Grandma Annie provided her observation. "And that Daniel and your other young friends are mighty handsome and charming," she added, peering over her glasses at Laura.

"Yes, Grandma, they are all real good people," Laura reassured her. "And I think your chocolate chips were their favorite cookies."

With a quizzical smile on her face, Grandma Annie just peered over the top of her glasses at Laura for a moment. She handed the bag of vegetables to Danielle and told Laura to bring in the watermelon. Laura's legs, arms, and hands were aching because they had really pushed hard this week to finish the harvest, but there was no way she was going to tell her grandma that she couldn't carry that watermelon into the kitchen. She sat on the top step and took off her shoes. Picking up the watermelon, Laura followed her grandma and Danielle into the kitchen.

SHOPPING, SHOPPING, AND MORE SHOPPING

It was Friday night, Laura had received her last pay and she wanted to make sure her money was straight. Having already set aside the last $40 allocation to her mama, Laura counted her remaining cash. She had $822! This was the most money she ever had, and Laura had a plan. She had taken a couple of small envelopes from the box in her mama's bedroom. She counted out $100 and put it in one of the small envelopes. Then Laura counted out $240 and put it in the second small envelope. She had $482 remaining in her large money envelope. She stood at the chest of drawer and thought to herself, that $482 was less than half of the $1,200 she originally planned on for clothes shopping money. But then Laura remembered that she had already spent practically her whole first $200 pay on clothes. Laura felt good. Standing there, she double-checked her counting in each envelope one more time. She then took the two small envelopes and the contact card from the three women and put them inside her large envelope along with the card with Daniel's phone number. If she could convince her mama to get a clothes dryer, it would be worth giving up the extra $240 shopping money. Laura put the large envelope, with everything inside, back under the neatly folded clothes in the top drawer. She closed the drawer and took a deep breath, letting out a sigh of relief. Laura had made it through the summer on the tobacco farm. Now it was time to shop!

It was going on 10:00 a.m., Saturday morning and Danielle's bed was empty. Laura had not even heard her lil sis get up; her body must have really needed that extra rest. Leisurely lying in the bed, Laura made a mental note to call Amy. She didn't want Amy to feel left out from their shopping plans. Laura and Sydney were planning to meet up on Sunday to review their lists and the advertisements. They were planning to go to the mall during the week when it was a little less crowded.

She did one final stretch and got up for the day. Coming down the hallway, Laura peeped into the living room and saw that Danielle was already parked in front of the television watching the Saturday morning cartoons. Continuing into the kitchen, surprisingly she found her mama already up and sitting at the kitchen table sipping a cup of coffee. The washing machine was humming along, already filled with a load of clothes. Laura had decided not to bring up the topic of buying a clothes dryer again until after she got the Sunday Sears advertisement from Sydney.

"Morning Mama." Laura said while getting a bowl out of the cabinet. She poured some cereal into the bowl and added just a tad bit of milk from the refrigerator. Laura didn't pour much milk in her cereal because it made it too soggy, and she liked the crunch of the cereal. She took a seat opposite her mama at the kitchen table.

Looking up from her coffee cup, her mama said, "You sure slept in late today."

"Yes," Laura responded. "I was really tired; yesterday was our last day working on the tobacco farm, and we worked extra hard all this week to get the harvest finished."

Laura gazed at her mama; she always seemed preoccupied, like you never really had her full attention.

Taking another sip of coffee, her mama said, "So, you and Sydney going to the mall today?"

"No," Laura responded. "We're going to wait and go during the week so we can shop when it's not too crowded."

The washing machine buzzed, signaling that the load of clothes was finished and ready to be hung out. Laura was finishing up the last of her cereal as her mama got up and walked toward the washing machine. She put the freshly washed clothes into the waiting laundry basket and put another waiting basket of dirty clothes into the washing machine. Laura knew that she still had to wash her dirty work clothes—for the last time.

About that time her mama said, "Laura, go ahead and get dressed so you can hang these clothes out on the line. I've got one more load to do, and then you need to wash all those work clothes."

"Yes, ma'am," Laura responded as she took her cereal bowl to the sink and quickly washed it.

Laura broodingly walked slowly down the short hallway back to her bedroom. She knew that her mama had a lot of things on her mind, but it would have been nice, she thought, for her mama to have at least said something positive about her having completed all six weeks on the tobacco farm. But then again, she reasoned to herself, her mama had never been out to the country, and because of their schedules, she had never once seen Laura coming in from work dirty and tired. Laura's mood lifted, and she laughed because her mama probably thought Laura, Sydney, and the other teens had a good time on the tobacco farm and really didn't work that hard. As Laura changed into a pair of shorts and t-shirt, she reflected that they really did have a good time, especially on Fridays, but they also really did work very, very hard. She walked back up the hallway to start hanging out the waiting load of wet clothes.

The rest of Saturday was pretty quiet and uneventful, which was just fine with Laura. She had pretty much spent the day hanging out clothes, bringing in clothes, and folding clothes. She also gave the bathroom a thorough cleaning, dusted the house, and cleaned their bedroom. Laura had plans for next week and didn't want any unfinished chores to interfere with Mama letting her go out.

Late evening, before the sun started to set, Laura and Sydney took Danielle to the schoolyard playground. The playground was almost empty, and there wasn't even a pickup softball game going on. That was unusual for a Saturday evening. Maybe everyone was taking a break from softball since the rec league season was over. The two teens took a seat on the bleachers, and Danielle went running off to the merry-go-round and swings.

"Girl, Mr. Isaiah and the guys met Grandma Annie yesterday. They all took an instant liking to her," Laura told Sydney.

"Well, your grandma is pretty easy to like," Sydney complimented. "She always makes me feel right at home."

It made Laura feel good to hear Sydney say those nice things about her grandma. The girls continued chatting, and their conversation naturally flowed to a discussion on school shopping. At Sunday dinner tomorrow, Laura was planning on finding out what days and hours her Aunt Nicky worked next week. The teens had reviewed the Kress ads and definitely decided to get their coats through Laura's Aunt Nicky. Sydney commented that she might also get a short jacket or big sweater from Kress. There were some nice ones in last week's Kress flyer.

Laura stood up and said, "Girl, my whole closet is from Kress. I worked in that tobacco all summer to get a new look." She started making posing motions for additional emphasis.

"OK, OK, I get it," Sydney assured her.

Laura began to laugh also at her own antics and sat back down on the bleacher. But she was still very serious about shopping for her school clothes at different stores.

"What do you think about all of us meeting up at the mall food court next Saturday?" Sydney asked, changing the subject from shopping.

"I can't wait! I honestly thought I wouldn't get to see Daniel until maybe a football game," Laura exclaimed with a big smile. "You know, we have never seen them and they have never seen us in regular clothes."

Thoughts of what to wear started dancing around in Laura's head. It was still pretty hot, but she definitely wanted to wear something other than jean shorts and a tank top, which was her normal weekend attire.

"Yeah, but all guys mostly wear jeans and t-shirts," Sydney interjected.

"Hey, Laura, come and push me on the swing," Danielle shouted, running up to them. Both girls got up and raced the lil girl back out to the swings. All three of them swung and played on the merry-go-round. It felt good to Laura and Sydney to play around like eight-year-olds for a little while as summer was rapidly ending. Walking back home, the girls talked about the approaching first day of school. Even Danielle was super excited about starting fourth grade. Change was coming like a slow breeze blowing through the air in the back of the big black shiny pickup truck on that first Monday morning when Mr. Isaiah drove them out to the tobacco farm.

Sitting on her front porch with all of the Sunday's advertisements and a few from last week's newspaper, Sydney was eagerly waiting for Laura to come review them with her. She spotted her best friend walking up the street. Laura greeted her with a big grin as she pulled her shopping list out of her shorts pocket. The girls huddled together on the porch plotting their week of school shopping. Laura had found out that Aunt Nicky was working Monday and Tuesday, off Wednesday, then working Thursday through Saturday. The girls decided to get their winter coats on Thursday before the weekend shopping crowd.

"Oh," Sydney said, "I talked to Amy at church today and told her about our shopping plans for the week. She said that she wants to go with us when we go to Kress. She wants to get a new winter coat."

"OK, cool," Laura responded. "But, girl, you know we can't all get the same coat and be walking around high school looking like triplets."

The girls were laughing so hard that Mrs. Wilson came out to check on them with two glasses of lemonade in hand. They planned to have their shopping done by Friday, because Saturday was going to be a fun day just hanging out with their new friends, especially Daniel. Before heading home, Laura took the new Sears appliance flyer, folded it up, and placed it in her pocket along with her shopping list.

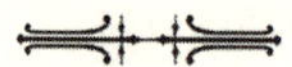

Laura and Sydney were up and at the mall each day, Monday through Wednesday, by 11:00 a.m. They had an absolute blast shopping. It was nothing like their first pay weekend when the teens just randomly made impulse purchases. They didn't openly carry their shopping lists from store to store, but it was definitely in their pockets for constant review while working their way from store to store buying new jeans, blouses, a couple of skirts, new sneakers, a pair of regular shoes, and a few accessories. The mall was not crowded at all, and they took their time selecting everything. Laura and Sydney were having such a good time that by Wednesday, they even decided to venture into K's, the teen clothing store where Carolyn and Brenda worked.

"Well, look who's in here on a Wednesday," Carolyn greeted them. "You two must be finished working in tobacco for the summer."

"Yep," Laura said as she kept right on walking past her to the rack of sundresses that were on sale.

Sydney just kept walking. The snide comments from the two girls no longer bothered Laura and Sydney as much as they did at the beginning of the summer.

K's was having a really great sale. All the sundresses were on sale for 70 percent off. Laura had been thinking about wearing a sundress on Saturday. She had bought one new sundress earlier in the summer, but she pondered getting another one since the sale was so good. She and Sydney looked through the rack of dresses. Laura chose a dark marigold-yellow sundress, it almost looked goldish instead of yellow. She held it up and looked at her reflection in the mirror. It looked real pretty against her skin.

"That one really looks nice," Sydney complimented her.

They looked through a couple more racks of dresses. Sydney also chose a sundress and a couple of blouses. The girls headed to the register and, of course, Brenda was working the register.

"Well, look who's here, you two spending that tobacco money?" Brenda commented as she rung up Laura's dress.

"Hi, yes, we're doing a little shopping," Laura greeted her while taking out her cash.

As Brenda rung up Sydney's items, she commented, "Oh, you all going to be twinning in these sundresses. They are cute though; I'm going to have to get a couple of them myself before they're all gone."

As the girls left the store with their purchases, Laura said to Sydney, "Can you believe her? Our sundresses are two completely different colors, and she talking about twinning! I see why my brother doesn't pay them any attention."

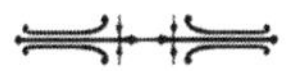

What a whirlwind shopping week! It was Thursday already, and Laura and Sydney were going to meet up with Amy to go downtown to the Kress store to pick out their winter coats. Laura's mama had agreed to let Danielle go with them since they were not going out to the mall. The girls had plans to also check out Roses and a few other local downtown shops. Laura was keeping close tabs on her spending and recalculating her cash every night. She had decided that with the coat sale and Aunt Nicky's discount, she had enough to get Danielle a new coat also.

Always enjoying the bus ride and watching the cars and people go by, Danielle was beyond excited. Laura clasped her lil sis's hand as they exited the bus and started walking up the street toward Kress. Danielle also reached for Sydney's hand. The four of them formed a line walking down the sidewalk, looking like the three teen musketeers plus one. Amy shared that she had purchased a few school clothes for her two younger brothers. They were going to the third and fifth grades. Danielle was going to the fourth grade. All the elementary kids went to the K-6 grade school at the top of the hill. Laura and Sydney had gone to the same school. They all joked about how everybody had turned the schoolyard into a summer playground and softball field.

From reviewing the Kress sales paper, the teen girls pretty much knew what coats they wanted to purchase. Laura had already alerted her Aunt Nicky that their friend Amy would be shopping with them, because she knew her aunt could sometimes be kinda loud. Danielle was like a kid in a candy store once Laura told her that she could pick out a new coat.

Aunt Nicky was on the lookout for them since Laura had told her they were planning to come into the store on Thursday. She spotted them around 11:30 a.m.

"Hey, girls, have you seen anything you like?" she greeted them.

"Oh, Aunt Nicky, look! Look!" Danielle squealed as she ran up and greeted her aunt with a coat in hand.

"So, you getting lil sis a coat too. You all must have really made some money on that tobacco farm!" she said, teasing the teen girls.

"Aunt Nicky, Danielle done tried on five coats, and she likes all of them," Laura said with a little exasperation in her voice.

"Well, let's see how they fit," Aunt Nicky said, bending down to help Danielle put her arms into the coat sleeve. The three teens were actually glad for the help; they let Aunt Nicky take charge of helping Danielle decide on a coat. It was almost 12:30 p.m. by the time all the coat selections were made. Aunt Nicky took their coats and told them that she will bring them to Laura's house later that evening whenever she got off from work.

"Wait for me while I go put these coats up," Aunt Nicky instructed them as she walked off toward the customer service area.

"This is really nice of your aunt," Amy pronounced.

"Yes, she's really saving us some money because these coats are our most expensive purchase other than the sneakers," Sydney confirmed.

After a few minutes, Aunt Nicky came back with her purse on her shoulder. "It's time for my lunch break," she announced. "Let's go down to Mae's Grill, you girls can treat me to lunch with some of that tobacco money."

"Where is my new coat?" Danielle asked Aunt Nicky.

The teen girls gave each other the eye.

"Well, I'm going to do a special delivery to your house this afternoon so that you don't have to carry that big coat on the bus," Aunt Nicky said with a wink, and she continued, "But right now how about a nice chocolate milkshake?"

"Yes!" Danielle exclaimed and joyfully took Aunt Nicky's hand as they headed toward the store's exit.

Laura watched the interaction and was a little surprised at how well her aunt handled Danielle's potential outburst. The girls were more than happy to treat Aunt Nicky to lunch. Laura found that her aunt was actually pretty cool to hang out with. She kept the girls laughing all through lunch. Mae's Grill made some of the best burgers in town.

"Well, I'll see you young folks later, some of us got to work more than just a summer for a living," Aunt Nicky said with teasing in her voice as they exited the diner.

She pulled one of Danielle's ponytails and said, "See you later, pretty girl."

Aunt Nicky turned to walk down the sidewalk toward Kress store. The girls walked around a little more, making a stop in Roses where Laura bought Danielle a new, slightly bigger Scooby-Doo backpack.

Leaving Roses, they walked in the direction of the bus transfer station and got there just in time to catch the 3:30 p.m. bus.

Getting off the bus, Laura checked her watch. It was almost 4:00 p.m., so she knew her mama was already at work. After that lunch of burger, fries, and a large chocolate milkshake, Danielle's stride had slowed down. At the bottom of the hill, Sydney and Amy said their goodbyes and kept walking straight towards the next intersection. Laura turned left down Pinewood Street holding her lil sis's hand to keep her moving.

Settling Danielle in front of the television for some afternoon cartoons, Laura went to the bedroom to relax and think about her approach for talking to her mama again about getting a clothes dryer. She had to talk to her tomorrow, Friday, because the appliance sale ended on Saturday. The sound of the phone ringing interrupted her thoughts.

"Who's calling this time of the day?" she said out loud while getting up to go into the living room.

Stepping into the hallway, Danielle met her with a big grin on her face. "It's Daniel," she announced. "Bye, Daniel, here's Laura," the lil girl said into the phone.

"Give me that," Laura said, taking the phone from her lil sis, stepping back into the bedroom, and closing the door. They hadn't talked but once over the weekend.

"Hi, Laura, you been enjoying your break?" Daniel's deep voice came through the phone like music to her ears.

"It's been good," Laura said while taking her two pillows and propping them up against the headboard. Leaning back on the pillows, she visualized his handsome dimpled face.

"Do you like living in the country?" she asked.

"I guess, I've never lived anywhere else," Daniel responded. "I'm really looking forward to coming into town and seeing you on Saturday."

"Me too," Laura said while twiddling with her hair, wondering how she was going to wear it on Saturday. She had worn it in one pulled-back ponytail all summer. "Who's bringing y'all into town?"

Daniel told her all about their transportation plans. His dad was going to drop them off at the mall on Saturday morning. They were still trying to work something out for a late evening pickup so they could stay in town all day. Football practice had already started for David Jr. so he couldn't drive them into Ervinsville. Laura could listen to his voice all day. The bedroom door opened, and Danielle poked her head inside. Laura pointed her finger toward the living room for her lil sis to go back and sit down. Danielle turned around but left the door ajar. They chatted for a few more minutes, then ended the call. Laura hung up the phone and sat it down on the bed. She pulled up her knees, rested her chin on them and thought about the summer and all that had happened in just six weeks. It had started out soo bleak with no job prospects. The whole summer had turned into an adventure beyond her imagination except she had actually lived it!

It was Friday morning, and Laura knew her mama usually got up around 10:00 a.m. Laura wanted to talk to her about the clothes dryer before she got rushed with cooking dinner and getting ready for work. She turned over and looked at the three plastic garment bags hanging on the back of the bedroom door and Danielle's hanging on the doorknob. Aunt Nicky had brought the coats over last night, and Laura was glad that she had rung the coats up on three separate tickets. It will make collection simple. Looking at the receipts last night, she saw that Aunt Nicky really did save them a lot of cash. She planned to deliver them to Sydney and Amy later today and collect the money.

After getting dressed and fixing Danielle a bowl of cereal, Laura put on some coffee to brew round 9:30 a.m. when she heard her mama get up and go into the bathroom. A few minutes later, wearing her big multicolor housecoat, she strolled into the kitchen and took a deep breath of the coffee aroma filling the kitchen.

"Ah, that smells good," her mama exclaimed and went straight to the cupboard to get her coffee mug.

Danielle was finishing up her cereal, and the second Mama sat down at the kitchen table, she began telling her all about their Thursday shopping day. Mama just let her talk while she smiled and nodded in between sips of coffee. Finally, Danielle stopped talking long enough to announce that she was going to get her new coat and show it to her. Down the hall she went. Laura picked up her empty cereal bowl and carried it to the sink.

"That was really nice of you to get your sister a new coat," her mama thanked Laura.

Laura blushed; she was glad that she could finally help.

Danielle came back into the kitchen wearing her new burgundy coat fully buttoned up, with the attached hood on her head and the new Scooby-Doo backpack on her arm. Laura and her mama burst into laughter at the sight of the lil fashionista on the hot August morning.

By the time Laura got back from visiting and delivering Sydney's and Amy's coats, it was around 2:00 p.m. Walking into the house, she could smell the fish sticks and fries in the oven. Danielle was perched in front of the television. Her mama was standing at the sink busily cutting up some cucumbers, tomatoes, and carrots for a salad. It wasn't often that Laura helped her mama in the kitchen, simply because they were rarely home at the same time. Even during the school year, her mama would leave a casserole or some other food already prepared. All Laura had to do was warm it up in the oven.

She walked up to the sink with hesitancy in her step and asked, "Mama, do you want me to help cutting up the vegetables?"

"No, I'm almost finished; hand me that bowl from the dishrack," her mama replied.

Laura took the plastic bowl and placed it on the kitchen counter next to the cutting board. Standing at the sink fidgeting with her hands, Laura took the Sears appliance ad out of her pocket and took a seat at the kitchen table. She started telling her mama all about how she had saved up most of her tobacco money until this week and had gotten some real good deals on her school clothes. Actually, her mama had not even seen any of the clothes Laura had purchased, except for Danielle's coat. Laura even told her about saving the hundred dollars for school activities.

"That's good, Laura," her mama responded while still cutting up the vegetables.

Laura knew her mama was only half listening. So, taking a deep breath, she said, "I know you don't think we need one, but I have set aside one week's pay to buy us a clothes dryer. We only have to use it on the weekends when it's raining or really freezing cold outside, so it shouldn't use up too much electricity. Tomorrow is the last day for the appliance sale at Sears."

Placing the vegetables in the bowl, her mama turned around. Oh, here it comes, Laura thought.

"Laura, your grandma told me that you've been asking a lot of questions about her clothes dryer; how much does she use it; how much does it increase her electric bill and so on." Her mama began tearing off pieces from a head of lettuce and adding it to the bowl of vegetables. She started talking again. "I'm really proud of you and how you stuck with working on the tobacco farm all summer to buy your school clothes, but when that money's gone, it's gone."

"But, Mama," Laura began.

Her mama stopped her and continued, "Let me finish. You can purchase the clothes dryer, but it can only be used for extreme weather days like freezing rain and snow."

Laura started to smile inside while still putting on a solemn face for the rest of the lecture.

Her mama continued, "You already know the electric bill is going to be higher in the winter. If that electric bill goes up too high, that clothes dryer is going to be unplugged and just become another piece of unused furniture in that corner."

"Yes, ma'am!" Laura declared exuberantly, jumping up and wrapping her arms around her mama. Laura almost knocked the bowl of salad off the counter.

"Girl, go check those fish sticks and fries in the oven," her mama uttered while gently pushing Laura away.

Laura knew that her mama was not one to show a lot of affection and different emotions. She was just kinda matter-of-factly in her actions, except with Aunt Nicky. She brought out the fun side of her mama. Laura breathed a sigh of relief as she took the tray of fish sticks and fries out of the oven. She didn't know if she was happier about the new school clothes or the clothes dryer.

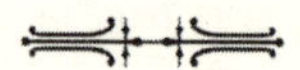

Later that night, Laura decided to set the alarm clock for 8:00 a.m. Time was going to be tight Saturday morning. She and Sydney had decided to catch the 10:00 a.m. bus downtown, then catch the 10:30 a.m. transfer to the mall. Amy was going to meet them at the food court around noon. Laura wanted to get to Sears and purchase the clothes dryer before meeting up with the crew in the food court. She was still elated that her mama had agreed to the purchase. It was the first time she had set the alarm clock since their last day on the tobacco farm. While setting the clock, she heard the phone ringing in the living room. She had already seen Sydney that afternoon, so maybe it was Daniel. Rushing down the short hallway, she reached up and brushed back her ponytail as if he were there in person.

Picking up the phone, she said, "Hello," with a smile on her face.

The voice on the other end answered back, "Hey, girl, guess what?"

"Hey, what happened?" Laura responded with a tad bit of disappointment that it wasn't Daniel's voice that greeted her on the other end of the phone.

Sydney said, "My dad's going to drop us at the mall tomorrow. Jacob was telling him about how we are meeting our friends from the tobacco farm at the food court tomorrow, and he said that he has to run an errand out that way, so he'll drop us. We'll pick you up around 10:40 a.m. because it won't take that long to get to the mall in the car."

"Oh, girl, that's great!" Laura responded. "Because I was already thinking about my hair sweating out and getting frizzy from walking up that hill tomorrow morning to the bus stop."

Both girls laughed and chatted for a few more minutes. Laura heard the front door opening; it was John. The girls ended their call and hung up the phones.

Cheerfully, Laura greeted John and told him all about their mama agreeing to getting the clothes dryer. John was not too surprised. He told Laura that Mama had told him that Grandma Annie told her that it was about time to get a clothes dryer because our clothes were getting too big to try to hang them up on that tiny bathroom shower rod to dry when the weather was bad.

"Thank you, Grandma Annie," Laura said out loud.

She and John both laughed. He took a seat beside Laura on the couch and said, "I saw Jacob and Mike at the ballfield today. They said that you all are meeting up with your tobacco farm friends at the mall food court tomorrow."

"Yes, we are," Laura answered pensively.

"And," John continued, "they said your friends are three guys, and one named Daniel seems to have a little crush on you."

"Sydney and Amy are going too," Laura quickly responded. "We're all going to meet up for lunch and then go to the matinee showing of that new *Smokey and the Bandit* movie that came out this week. Then we're going to ride the bus back home and maybe catch a game at the park ballfield."

Laura gave her brother the full plan for the day, wanting to reassure him that it was a group event. Since the guys played softball with him, she knew that eventually John would hear about Daniel.

"OK, it's cool cause Jacob and Mike said they'll be there. And Eric said he may see you all at the park ballfield after he gets off from work. I'm working tomorrow until closing at the grocery store," John said, looking directly at Laura.

"Don't worry, I'll be home long before then. You know I have to be home before dark," Laura assured her brother.

"OK, have fun," John stated, bringing the conversation to a close as he redirected his attention to flipping through the channels on the television.

"Thanks, good night," Laura said as she got up and walked back to her bedroom, wondering which pair of earrings would go best with her new sundress.

THE MEETUP

Laura reached over and turned off the alarm clock. She had set the alarm because she wanted to wake up early to have uninterrupted time in the bathroom. But no need for it today because Laura was wide awake. She lay there for a few more minutes, thinking about the day ahead. Today was going to be the first time Daniel ever saw her in real clothes and not those tobacco work clothes. She wondered what he was going to wear—probably jeans and a t-shirt. She hadn't talked to Daniel since he called on Thursday night. Laura still had not worked up the courage to call his house.

According to the weather report, it was going to be another steamy hot August Saturday. Laura decided to style her hair in the usual ponytail but with loosely curled pieces of hair framing the front of her face. She was finishing curling her hair when Danielle came into the bathroom. The lil girl admiringly complimented Laura on her curls. Smiling at her reflection in the bathroom mirror, Laura thanked her lil sis. Putting the curling iron away, Laura told Danielle to brush her teeth while she went and fixed her some cereal.

Laura was kinda hoping her mama would sleep in just a little later this morning. She sat and ate a quick bowl of Frosted Flakes with Danielle and then got her settled in front of the television to watch Saturday morning cartoons. Laura was really trying to keep Danielle as quiet as possible while she went back to the bedroom to finish getting dressed.

Looking at herself in the mirror, Laura really liked the way the bright marigold hoop earrings framed her face with the curls dangling down. They really sparkled and matched perfectly with her marigold yellow sundress, especially against her evenly tanned dark-hued skin. Laura decided to wear her white sandals with the little gold buckles on top. Taking one last glance in the mirror, Laura thought the whole ensemble looked really cute. She put her lip gloss into her small crossbody purse, glanced at the clock, and started down the hallway.

"Morning, Mama," Laura said, stopping to stand just outside the kitchen doorway and poking her head inside.

She really didn't want to go all the way into the kitchen.

Her mama, turning around from the coffee pot and seeing Laura, said, "You're pretty dressed up for a Saturday at the mall."

"I haven't worn anything this summer except blue jean pants or jean shorts, so I decided to wear one of my new sundresses today. Sydney's dad is going to drop us at the mall." Laura explained while not moving from the kitchen entryway.

"Well, you look very pretty," her mama said while still standing at the kitchen counter adding sugar to her cup of coffee.

Laura wished her mama would sit down at the kitchen table, the standing at the counter was making her nervous. She wanted to get to the mall early to go to Sears to purchase the clothes dryer. Laura had not told her mama that she and Sydney were meeting up with their friends from the tobacco farm at the mall. She didn't want her mama to hear about it from John.

"Oh," Laura said, stepping just inside the kitchen. "We're also meeting some friends from the tobacco farm at the mall food court. They're coming into town to do some school shopping."

"Daniel's coming to town," Danielle blurted out, walking past Laura into the kitchen.

Her mama took a sip of coffee, tilted her head to the left, and asked, "Who's Daniel?"

"Laura's tobacco friend; he's nice," Danielle clarified for their mama.

Laura felt as if sweat was starting to pour down her face and all the curls were starting to frizz up around her forehead and temple.

"He's one of the friends we're meeting up with. Grandma and Danielle met them last Friday when they helped drop off the watermelon and vegetables," Laura explained.

Not moving from the counter and peering straight at Laura, her mama said with firmness in her voice, "So, this is not a date because you know that you're not allowed to date yet."

"No, ma'am, this is not a date; me, Sydney, Jacob, and the others who worked on the tobacco farm with us are just meeting up with our new friends that we made over the summer," Laura affirmed.

Her mama stood there staring at Laura for a few seconds. To Laura it felt like hours.

Then she said, "OK, have fun and be home before it gets dark."

The firm, stern look was still set in her eyes as she took another sip of coffee. Not a moment too soon for Laura, they heard a car horn, but couldn't see who it was from the kitchen window. Danielle was on the move again, running to look out the living room window.

"That must be Mr. Wilson," Laura stated and turned to go check as her mama finally took a seat at the kitchen table.

She was glad to be out of that kitchen and away from her mama's piercing eyes.

"It's Sydney!" Danielle announced.

Laura opened the door, and Sydney was walking up to the porch, also wearing one of her new sundresses. She quickly let Sydney know that she was coming out. Danielle peeped her head out the door from around Laura.

"Hey, squirt," Sydney grinned and waved at the lil girl.

Laura walked back to the kitchen and quickly confirmed to her mama that it was indeed Mr. Wilson, Sydney, and Jacob.

Her mama looked up from sitting at the kitchen table, coffee cup still in hand, and said "OK, I'll see you this afternoon."

Laura quickly headed for the front door before any more questions came up.

Danielle was looking out the living room window and shouted, "Bye, Laura, you look pretty!"

Laura smiled and winked at her lil sis. Danielle giggled as her attention turned back to the Saturday morning cartoons. Maybe I'll pick something up for the lil tattletale, Laura thought as she exited the front door and walked to the car with a very, very happy pep in her step.

Mr. Wilson dropped them off in front of the food court entrance just before 11:00 a.m. Jacob headed for the sneaker store where Eric worked. Amy had already told them that she and Mike would meet them around noon at the food court. Not wanting everybody in her family's business, Laura was glad that it was just her and Sydney. They started walking in the direction of Sears. It was early, but the mall was already getting crowded. Laura saw a few familiar faces as they strolled down the long walkway, but the girls didn't stop to talk to anyone. Sears was all the way down on the opposite end of the mall from the food court.

The Sears appliance salesman approached the two teen girls with reserved courtesy. But he soon found out that Laura was very serious about purchasing a clothes dryer. She had the sales advertisement and knew exactly which one she wanted to buy. Laura made the purchase and set up the delivery for next Wednesday, August 27th. Thank goodness they were in the mile radius for free delivery because she had calculated the tax but not any delivery charges.

With the clothes dryer purchase finalized, Laura and Sydney started their stroll back down the opposite side of the mall toward the food court. It was getting close to noon, and Laura was starting to feel a little nervous. As they approached Claire's accessory store, Sydney wanted to make a quick stop. Sydney loved all the cute accessories in that store and could never walk past it without wanting to go inside. Laura glanced at her watch, they had about twenty-five minutes, so she agreed to stop because they were just a few shops down from the food court area. The teens browsed around the store. The store had so many different types of earrings, bracelets, and hair accessories to look at that you could really lose track of time. Laura picked up a couple more sets of barrettes and hair ribbons for Danielle. Glancing at her watch again, she saw that it was ten minutes before noon. Not wanting to be late meeting the others, Laura ushered Sydney to the check out.

The food court had gotten much more crowded than when they initially came into the mall, but Laura and Sydney immediately spotted their friends at a round table in the back corner location. Laura saw everybody right off, and why was Eric at the table? she pondered. She and Sydney greeted the group almost simultaneously as they approached the table. But Laura's eyes clearly rested on Daniel's face with that ready, dimpled smile. He stood up to greet them and grabbed two chairs from the next table while everybody was saying their hellos. Laura saw that Daniel was wearing a pair of blue jeans with a black tank-style t-shirt and a black-and-red button-down short-sleeve shirt with all the buttons undone. Glancing up and down quickly, she saw that he was also wearing a pair of very clean white sneakers with black and red stripes. Daniel had topped his look off with a fresh haircut. He even seemed taller and more strikingly handsome, if that was even possible. Wow, he was well put together!

Daniel placed the two empty chairs beside his chair and announced, "Y'all can sit here."

Laura didn't miss Daniel's eyes quickly scanning her from head to toe as she took the seat beside him. Laura wondered what Daniel thought about her appearance. Sydney took the other empty seat beside Laura.

"I ran into Daniel and Anthony in the sneaker store, and we've been hanging out. Eric walked down here with us," Jacob told the girls.

"Yep, but I got to head back to work in a few minutes," Eric interjected.

Laura wondered if Eric was just trying to check out their new friends at the request of her brother. He always seemed to be around.

"Well, I'm hungry. It's time to get something to eat," Anthony announced as he stood up to walk toward the hamburger stand.

"OK, maybe I'll catch up with you guys later," Eric said, turning to walk back toward the mall shopping area.

Mike and Amy got up along with the others to go purchase food. Amy was wearing a multicolored sundress. Laura decided to stay back and hold their table because she was too nervous to even think about food. Everyone walked toward the food stands, but Daniel stayed back.

He lightly touched Laura's shoulder to get her attention and said, "I'll bring something back for you; what do you want?"

Keenly aware of his hand on her bare shoulder, Laura managed to stammer out, "Ah, I'm not really hungry, just a small soda and fries, thanks."

"OK, I got it," he said with that smile and walked toward the food stands.

After giving her order, Sydney came back and sat at the table with Laura. Her brother, Jacob, was going to bring her food back to the table.

"Girl, Daniel was really checking you out!" Sydney exclaimed while they were sitting alone at the table.

"Is my hair messed up; we should have stopped in the restroom on our way down here; I completely forgot to put on some lip gloss!" Laura blurted out all in succession.

"Girl, did you not see the smile on his face when you walked up; nothing but teeth!" Sydney said.

Both girls caught a fit of giggles as Sydney imitated Daniel's grin. Everyone started to return to the table with their food. Watching Daniel walk toward her carrying the tray of food with his deeply tanned, muscular arms protruding from the short-sleeve shirt made

Laura almost forget that the others were even there and that this was a group outing. Jacob and Mike had also gotten really toned with more muscles since working on the tobacco farm, but Laura clearly had her eyes only on Daniel. When he sat down with the food, Daniel adjusted his chair and was now sitting even closer to Laura without actually touching her. Laura's nostrils woke up because he smelled as good as he looked.

The roundtable conversation reminded Laura of their tobacco farm lunch breaks under the teen tree. The guys were talking about the upcoming football season and their favorite teams. David Jr. had already started high school football practice. The teen girls were discussing some of their shopping excursions. Laura looked around the table. They had all become really good friends. Even though it had only been a week since their last day on the tobacco farm, she missed listening to and talking with the group of teens. But what she didn't miss was stringing and looping that tobacco. Everyone was enjoying themselves, and the time seemed to fly by just like the lunch breaks under the tobacco farm teen tree. Even though Laura was fully aware that Jacob and Mike probably had instructions from John, to keep a watchful brotherly eye on her.

"Oh, it's almost 1:40 p.m.," Mike announced. "We'd better get out to the bus stop to catch the 2:00 p.m. bus downtown so we don't miss the movie."

The guys picked up the food trays and their bags. Daniel and Anthony had sneaker bags with another bag stuffed inside. Jacob also had a sneaker bag. Laura offered to hold Daniel's bag for him while he dumped the tray.

"You look beautiful," Daniel complimented Laura as he handed her the bag.

The bus ride downtown was fun with the continuation of talking and laughter. The guys were talking about the Pontiac Firebird Trans-Am

from the first *Smokey and the Bandit* movie. They were really looking forward to the movie. Laura and Sydney were sitting together, and Daniel and Anthony had sat right behind them. Laura was hoping the back of her hair and ponytail had not frizzed up. It should be OK, she thought, because they hadn't really walked outside today. She pondered if this was Daniel and Anthony's first time on the city bus. She'll have to ask Daniel later. The city bus had been her family's primary mode of transportation her whole life. There were a few stops along the way, so by the time the bus pulled into the downtown transfer station, it was almost 2:30 p.m.

Walking down the sidewalk toward the movie theater, Daniel positioned himself to the outside of the sidewalk and took Laura's hand into his. Laura looked to her right and touched her elbow to Sydney's arm to get her attention. Sydney nodded her head at Laura and smiled. They were walking in rows with Jacob and Anthony in the lead, Mike and Amy in the middle, then Daniel, Laura, and Sydney taking up the rear. Laura was sure they were catching some curious eyes, and she was seriously hoping they would not bump into Aunt Nicky. By the time they purchased snacks and took their seats in the theater, the previews for upcoming movies were starting to play. Mike and Amy walked to the end of the row and sat together; Daniel followed them, leaving one empty seat between him and Mike; he then took a seat and Laura sat beside him. Sydney sat on the other side of Laura, then Jacob left an empty seat between him and Sydney before taking a seat; finally, Anthony followed suit, leaving an empty seat between him and Jacob. They took up a whole row of seats with room to relax and watch the movie comfortably. The theater was not crowded, probably because most people were still at the mall shopping.

Could the day get any better? Laura sighed as she leaned back and finally relaxed. Watching the movie, she knew this was a group outing, but it sure felt like a date. Not that she would know what a date felt like, because she had never been on one. The movie was hilarious, and they all had some good laughs. At some point during the movie, Daniel started holding her hand again. His hands were much bigger and felt firm yet gentle against Laura's tiny hand. Laura had been sure to lotion her hands every evening all summer to keep them from getting rough from handling the tobacco. She hoped he liked the feel of her hand in his, because his hand made her feel calm and excited all at the same time. The movie ended and the lights came up. Laura glanced at her watch, and it was 5:10 p.m. Everybody stood up and stretched; Daniel let go of her hand and reached for his bag that he had placed in the seat in the row in front of them. Darn bag, Laura thought.

Stepping outside the theater, Sydney said, "Hey, we have just enough time to catch the 5:30 p.m. bus back to the neighborhood."

"Y'all sure live by that bus schedule," Daniel whispered in Laura's ear.

"It operates like clockwork, just like Mr. Isaiah," she teasingly whispered back.

They both laughed at their own private joke as the seven teens walked back down the street toward the bus transfer station. Again, Daniel walked to the outside of the sidewalk, holding Laura's hand. Since they'd met up in the food court, he had pretty much been holding Laura's hand all day. The city bus was a little more crowded, but they all still managed to sit together. After a few stops, the bus pulled up at the top of the hill.

Exiting the bus, Jacob explained to Daniel and Anthony that the schoolyard ballfield was right at the bottom of the hill, but the ballpark was a little farther away.

"OK, but we don't have enough time to play a pickup softball game today," Anthony responded as they all started to walk down the hill. He continued, "Mr. Isaiah is helping with some work at his church in town today, and we're catching a ride home with him."

"Yeah, he's going to pick us up at 7:00 p.m., and it's around 6:00 p.m. now," Daniel chimed in.

"OK, my dad's doing some work at the church also. He was going to the hardware store after dropping us off at the mall this morning. They're probably still there, so we can walk to my house and chill until Mr. Isaiah comes," Jacob suggested.

"Oh, I asked Mr. Isaiah to pick us up at Laura's grandma's house," Daniel spoke up. "I hope you don't mind," he directed to Laura.

Her mouth responded, "That's cool."

But her brain screamed, please don't let nobody be there except Grandma. By this time, they were halfway down the hill and saw the ballfield was empty. There were only a few kids playing on the swings. Laura was relieved because she didn't necessarily want an encounter with Carolyn and Brenda and their sarcastic mouths. But if they did run into them, she knew that with Jacob and Mike present, those girls would be seriously putting on the charm. When they reached the end of the hill, instead of turning to go down Pinewood Street toward Laura's house, they all kept walking straight toward the intersection for Timberwood Street. Daniel and Anthony were already familiar with the street from riding in with Mr. Isaiah on their last workday.

They made the left turn onto Timberwood and Amy's house was the first one the group reached. Laura and the group stopped to talk in front of Amy's house for a few minutes. Mike informed them that the county fair was starting Labor Day week and suggested that they plan to meet up again at the fairgrounds. Everybody was excited about the idea of a group outing to the fair. The fair always had free admissions night for students either on Friday or Saturday.

"OK, we'll coordinate because we always come into Ervinsville for the fair," Daniel enthusiastically said as he reached up and let his hands rest on the center of Laura's back.

"Cool, we've already got each other's phone numbers. See y'all later," Amy said as she turned to walk toward her porch.

Mike touched her arm and said, "I'll see you later."

Laura and Sydney looked at each other and smiled. Mike only lived a few houses down from Amy. But as the group approached his house, he kept right on walking with them, continuing in the discussion about the upcoming football season with Jacob and Anthony. Daniel, Laura, and Sydney walked just a few steps behind them. With stopping to talk at Amy's house and leisurely walking down the street, it was getting close to 6:30 p.m. by the time they reached Jacob and Sydney's house.

"Hey, do y'all want to wait here while I put my stuff up?" Jacob said, holding up his sneaker bag. "We can see Mr. Isaiah when he turns the corner toward Laura's grandma's house."

Anthony and Mike agreed to wait and walked up the steps, taking a seat on the porch.

Laura noticed that Mr. Wilson's car was not in the driveway. So, he and Mr. Isaiah were probably still at the church.

"Hey, Laura, since we've been gone all day, I'm going to go inside and check on my mom." Sydney said, then directed to Mike and Anthony. "You guys want some lemonade?"

"Sure," the guys responded in unison.

"Well, let's keep walking to your grandma's house," Daniel said. "It's only a few more houses, and we can wait on her porch for Mr. Isaiah."

The young teens continued to walk down the street holding hands. The house seemed quiet as they approached the porch. Laura looked at her watch; it read 6:40 p.m., and she knew if Mr. Isaiah told the guys he was picking them up at 7:00 p.m. then he would be there at precisely 7:00 p.m. They walked up the steps and sat down in the two porch rocking chairs. Grandma Annie had a small table in between the two chairs. This was the farthest the two teens had been apart since meeting up in the mall food court.

"You really do look pretty today," Daniel said, leaning forward in the white rocking chair.

"Thanks," Laura coyly smiled. "We both clean up pretty nice," she added teasingly.

Daniel laughed while reaching his hand across the table, touching her hair right along her temple. Laura blushed, because all day long she had been wondering what he thought about her outfit and hair as compared to her work outfit of oversized jeans and t-shirt with a bandana tied around her head. She was glad he couldn't see her blushing beneath her deeply tanned face.

"You look very handsome yourself with that fresh cut," Laura complimented him.

"Well, thank you, ma'am," Daniel teased and rubbed the top of his head.

They both burst out into a fit of laughter.

"I thought I heard some noise out here," Grandma Annie said, opening the screen door. With her glasses pushed down to the tip of her nose, she peered over them at Daniel and greeted him, saying, "Well, hello, handsome, you back again?"

"Yes, ma'am," Daniel responded, giving her that megawatt smile with dimples popping out everywhere.

Grandma Annie stepped completely out onto the porch, closing the screen door behind her. Mesmerized for a moment by Daniel's smile, Laura quickly came back to her senses and started to explain the day to her grandma. She explained how all the friends from the tobacco farm hung out together, going to the mall and then to the matinee. She continued talking with a slight hint of nervousness in her voice, telling her grandma all about the bus ride home and that Daniel and their other friend Anthony were waiting for Mr. Isaiah to pick them up any minute.

"Well, with all the day's activities and walking from the top of the hill, do you all want some tea, lemonade, or Kool-Aid while you wait?" Grandma Annie asked.

"No, thank you," they said in unison.

Laura thought with them not wanting anything to drink, her grandma would go back inside. But not Grandma Annie, she was having too much fun teasing the young teens.

"Doesn't my granddaughter look pretty in her sundress? I don't think I've seen her in too much of nothing this summer but big, oversized, boy-looking clothes," Grandma Annie said, peering over her glasses.

Daniel couldn't help himself, he burst out laughing and said, "Yes, ma'am, that's all I've seen her in until today, but she's pretty no matter what she's wearing."

"Yes, she is!" Grandma Annie agreed with a smile and wink over the top of her glasses.

Laura was sitting there wishing the porch would swallow her up. She felt like her whole body was one big, blushing fire.

"Grandma, please!" she said with an exacerbated grin.

Grandma Annie laughed good-heartedly and touched Laura on her shoulders, reassuring her that it was just good-natured teasing. Laura already knew her grandma could be a handful. She was just thankful that Aunt Nicky nor her mama were there. Daniel rubbed the top of his head and smiled as he watched Laura and her grandma interact.

About that time, they saw Mr. Isaiah's gleaming, big black truck make the left turn down the street, heading straight for Grandma Annie's house.

"Good afternoon, ma'am," Mr. Isaiah bellowed from the cab of the truck.

Laura glanced at her wristwatch and inwardly smiled; it was 7:00 p.m.

Grandma Annie continued with the charm, greeting Mr. Isaiah and thanking him again for the fresh vegetables and watermelon, assuring him that everything was delicious. Mr. Isaiah smiled broadly as Laura and Daniel stood up and started to walk down the steps. Mr. Isaiah was getting ready to ask about Anthony's whereabouts when they saw him running down the street toward them.

"These young folks done had themselves one fun-filled day spending that tobacco money!" Grandma Annie hollered to Mr. Isaiah from the porch.

The two adults laughed at the light teasing.

"Hey," Anthony said, reaching the truck. "Hi, Laura's Grandma Annie!" he shouted to the elderly lady standing on the porch.

"Hey, young fella," she greeted him back.

Anthony got into the cab of the truck and moved over so that Daniel could get in also.

While all this was going on, Daniel and Laura stood awkwardly on the sidewalk near the truck. Speaking softly to Laura, he said, "I had a really good time today, and my mom said to tell you not to be afraid to call the house."

"Come on, Daniel," Anthony yelled from inside the truck.

"Yep, we'd better get moving, it's after seven o'clock. Bye, ma'am," Mr. Isaiah bellowed from the truck.

"Bye, you all be safe driving home," Grandma Annie shouted back.

As the adults were exchanging goodbyes, Daniel bent down and, ever so swiftly, lightly kissed Laura on her lips and said, "Bye, I'll call you later."

It happened so fast that Laura just stood there in awe as Daniel jumped in the truck. She waved and watched the truck go down the street and make the right turn at the corner.

It was her very first kiss! Suddenly, Laura remembered that Grandma Annie was still standing on the porch. Hopefully, she was so engrossed in talking to Mr. Isaiah that she didn't see the kiss!

Not moving from the very spot Daniel had kissed her, Laura turned around and announced, "Grandma, guess what, Mama agreed, and I bought the clothes dryer today. They're going to deliver it on Wednesday!"

"That's great," her grandma responded, still standing at the top of the steps.

Laura knew her grandma rarely missed anything with those keen eyes peering over the top of her glasses.

"Aw, well, it's getting late, I'd better get home. I'll see you tomorrow morning for church," Laura said while waving and turning to walk up the street. She didn't want to prolong the conversation with her grandma.

Walking home slowly, Laura wanted to savor every minute of the day. She skipped up the steps and opened the front door. Danielle jumped off the couch, greeting her and eagerly asking if her big sis had brought her something from the mall. Laura could hear her mama in the kitchen, probably prepping the chicken for Sunday dinner.

"Hey, Mama, I'm back," Laura hollered into the kitchen.

"OK, hope you had fun with your friends. It's starting to get dark, so go bring in that last load of clothes," her mama responded.

Without even taking time to change, Laura walked into the kitchen and picked up the laundry basket by the back door. Nothing, not even bringing in yet another load of clothes could ruin this day. Danielle was right behind her and followed Laura outside to help bring in the laundry before the streetlights came on.

It wasn't even 9:30 p.m. yet, but Laura found herself in Danielle's bed with the lil girl sound asleep, snuggled into her side. She eased out, not wanting to wake her lil sis. Laura walked to the dresser and picked up her crossbody purse and took out $55. She left the change in the little coin purse. Opening the top drawer of the chest of drawer, she took out her money envelope and put the cash in the small envelope with the remaining $100. Laura felt a real sense of accomplishment about how she had spent her hard-earned $1,200. She even had managed to save over half of one pay for school activities...including the county fair, she smiled to herself.

Still standing there, Laura then picked up the card with Daniel's phone number and stared at it as she remembered first seeing him on the back of the tobacco truck in dirty overalls with that dimpled smile. She had an instant attraction to him, and wow did he look handsome today all cleaned up! Staring at the card, Laura thought, I need to call Sydney and tell her about the kiss! Her mama was in the living room watching television and it was getting late, so Laura decided to forego calling Sydney until tomorrow. Maybe I'll also call Daniel tomorrow, Laura contemplated as she put the card back in the money envelope, placed it under her clothes, and closed the drawer.

Sitting in the dark, propped up on her pillows, Laura pondered all that had happened over the summer, from Sydney's family knowing Mr. Isaiah and him offering them the opportunity to work on the tobacco farm up until this very great Saturday. Who would have thought so much change could happen over one summer in just six weeks. She had new school clothes that actually fit her body. But Laura had also decided to go through the clothes from Aunt Nicky and pick out a few pieces. She had definitely learned some money prudency over the summer from listening to Mrs. Mary, Mrs. Cindy, and Miss Elaine. Laura sighed deeply; she was going to miss those women from the tobacco farm and their lively conversations. It was like having a whole new community of friends, even though they lived thirty miles away out in the country. And, of course, all the advice from Grandma Annie and how she helped convince her mama to agree to letting her purchase the clothes dryer. That purchase was better than any new school clothes. Well, not quite better, but a very close second, Laura laughed to herself.

Pulling her knees up and leaning her chin forward, Laura smiled to herself thinking about the upcoming county fair. It opened Labor Day Monday. Laura already knew that she and Daniel were going to have a blast riding everything at the fairgrounds, especially the roller coaster.

That week would also be her first week of high school. Laura leaned back against the pillows. She was drifting off to sleep with thoughts of starting high school when the sound of the phone ringing startled her back fully awake.

"Laura, it's Sydney," her mama shouted down the hallway.

Laura glanced at the clock as she got up and went down the short hallway. It was after 10:00 p.m.; Sydney never called that late. Not wanting to talk in front of her mama, she picked up the whole phone and started back down the hallway. Going into the bathroom and closing the door, Laura was excited to tell Sydney about the kiss!

"Hey, girl, you're not going to believe what happened this afternoon," Laura began.

But before she could continue, Sydney interrupted with "Girl, listen, I have got to tell you something!

"But today," Laura started again.

"No, you have got to hear this." Sydney continued.

"What?" Laura asked with heightened concern in her voice.

You know how Eric always seems to be around or showing up wherever we are? Well! According to my brother, Eric likes you!" Sydney declared.

"What! No way!" Laura responded in utter astonishment. "He likes you!"

Sydney continued, "Jacob said that Eric hasn't said anything to you because he's a junior. He didn't want any grief from your brother, John, since you were still in junior high."

"Girl, no way!" was all Laura could manage to say as all the random encounters with Eric this summer started to play back in her head.

"Listen," Sydney said, "remember how he always came around when we were at the school playground, and when you didn't come to the final rec league softball game, he specifically asked me about you."

"But..." Still in disbelief, Laura chimed in. "He walked you home a few times."

"Girl, please!" Sydney retorted. "We were just going in the same direction. You know he lives over on Pinecone Road, which is one street over." Sydney laughed and continued, "Besides I told you he always stopped and talked softball with Jacob. After our meetup today, Jacob just told me tonight that when they were playing a pickup game of softball last week, Eric heard them talking about meeting up with their new friends from the tobacco farm and how one of them, Daniel, had taken a liking to you. That's when Eric spoke up about liking you also. Your brother wasn't at the ballfield that day. They told him later about the meetup and Daniel liking you. Girl, that's why Eric came down to the food court, checking out you and the competition." Sydney giggled.

Laura's head was spinning; she sat down on the closed toilet seat lid. She only saw Eric as one of her brother's friends from the neighborhood. Not only that, but she was absolutely positive that he had taken a liking to Sydney!

"But listen to this," Sydney continued talking. "Jacob told me that Eric wants to ask you to go to the county fair with him."

"Oh no way!" Laura almost screamed incredulously in an elevated tone. "We're doing a group day at the fair with Daniel and them!"

"Laura, everything all right in there?" Her mama shouted down the hallway from the living room.

She opened the bathroom door and shouted, "Yes, ma'am, I'm just talking to Sydney."

Laura closed the bathroom door and lowered her voice. "Girl, I'm not interested in no Eric. Didn't you see how attentive and handsome Daniel was today?"

"Yeah, but I bet Eric will either invite himself to go with us or just happen to show up at the fairgrounds on the same day that we're all there," Sydney said with a bit of sarcasm in her voice.

"Ugh!" Laura screeched.

Still in shock and disbelief, she and Sydney decided to meet up tomorrow after church to talk. Laura hung up the phone and just sat there on the toilet seat cover for a minute.

Ah! I didn't even tell Sydney about the kiss, my first kiss, Laura thought as she stood up, glanced in the mirror, took a deep breath, and opened the bathroom door. She slowly walked down the short hallway carrying the phone. Maybe Jacob misunderstood the conversation, but that would be one huge misunderstanding. Laura was still convinced that Eric liked Sydney. She placed the phone back on the little table in the living room.

Her mama looked up from the television and asked, "Is everything OK with you and Sydney? She called kinda late."

Lost in thought, Laura barely heard her mama's question. "Yes, ma'am, everything's fine." Laura responded as she walked slowly back down the hallway to her bedroom.

"The week had been so perfect...new school clothes...a new clothes dryer...and especially spending Saturday with Daniel!" "Now this!" Laura muttered incredulously to herself. Laura didn't care if Daniel did go to a different high school in another town thirty miles away and Eric was from the neighborhood. Daniel made her laugh, their conversations flowed easily, and he was so handsome. Laura sat down on her twin bed visualizing Daniel standing up to greet her in the food court today. She couldn't help but smile. Nope, there must be a mistake. Laura leaned back on her bed pillows and mused—only one more week of summer break and she would be starting high school. Her first year of high school was going to be very intriguing!

Made in the USA
Middletown, DE
08 July 2024